AGYAR

STEVEN BRUST,

P.J.F.

TOR
fantasy®

A TOM DOHERTY ASSOCIATES BOOK
NEW YORK

AGYAR

Copyright © 1993 by Steven Brust

A Tor Book
Published by Tom Doherty Associates, Inc.
175 Fifth Avenue
New York, N.Y. 10010

Edited by Terri Windling

Library of Congress Cataloging-in-Publication Data

Brust, Steven.
     Agyar : Steven Brust.
         p. cm.
     "A Tom Doherty Associates book."
     ISBN 0-312-85178-2
     I. Title.
     PS3552.R84A73   1993
     813'.54—dc20   92-39747
                                                CIP

First edition: March 1993

Printed in the United States of America

0 9 8 7 6 5 4 3 2 1

For Will and Emma
And the stuff we make of dreams

ACKNOWLEDGMENTS

I would like to offer my sincere thanks to the following people:

Dr. Flash Gordon and Betsy Pucci for medical assistance and information.

Maria Pinkstaff, for advice on ritual magic.

Emma Bull, Kara Dalkey, Pamela Dean, Will Shetterly, and David Dyer-Bennet for much helpful criticism.

Terri Windling for editing.

Lt. Ed Nuquist of the Minneapolis Police Department, for help with police procedure.

Neil Gaiman, my Evil Twin, for showing me that beauty can lie in places I'd never thought to look for it.

And my brother-in-law, Tom, for starting it all by talking about Dickens when it was much too late at night for such things.

PROLOGUE

I feel the need to write something more before I go on my way, something that can go on top of this pile of papers, and the last shall be first, as someone or other said in a different context.

It has been several days since I've been up in this little room, and in that time spring has come on with a vengeance. There's a little joke for you, lover. But I don't feel much like laughing. Since I was here last, I read this—what? What shall I call it? Collection of typed pages, I suppose. I read it, and it did to me what I hadn't thought could be done any more.

For the love of love, how many changes can take place in a person before it all becomes meaningless and there is nothing left but a sort of numbness? Is that where I am now? No. Just the opposite; it is more like pins and needles of the soul.

Hmmm. Not bad. Do you like that turn of phrase, lover?

Lover.

There is something ironic in the way I've been using that word, and that isn't right. There is irony aplenty, but not there, and in writing to myself, and to you, I ought not to hide behind the pretense.

I don't know why reading these papers has made such a difference, unless it's just that I hadn't known before what you were thinking and feeling all this time. I knew what you did; I didn't know why, and that seems to matter, though it flies in the face of reason. Even a few days ago, when I was last in this room, I thought all of these emotions were dead, and now they are in my face, coexisting with a hungerlike pain.

But that, I suppose, is the answer. I cannot deny the hunger; I will not deny the feelings, either. Does it really matter what you feel when you do something? Does it somehow make a difference if you're sorry when you go blasting your way over someone's life like a locomotive over a papier-mâché doll?

How about that one, my love?

Yes, I think it does matter. We do what we have to do, and if we learn regret, than that, too, matters, or so I now believe. I will take these papers with me, and I will also take those poems that are sitting in my room below, and I will leave, as planned, and live, as planned, and read this again. Maybe I'll arrange it all nice and neat, divide it into chapters, and put quotes from Shakespeare or something in front of each, and send it off somewhere. Perhaps if I read it again I will understand it a little better, although, come to that, I didn't enjoy reading it the first time; it reminded me more than anything of looking into a mirror when I was fifteen and bothered by acne.

Maybe that's it; maybe I have acne in my soul.

I shouldn't joke about it, because it really isn't

funny. I saw myself, and I didn't like what I saw. Can I do anything about it?

I know that you did.

Everything has melted, and spring, with her warm breeze slipping through the boards over the window, has created her own metaphor; that of tears from the melting heart. Two days ago I could not have written that with a straight face, and now I cannot bring myself to laugh, and that is your fault. Did you know what you were doing when you put this here for me to read?

I asked if I could change, and now, twenty minutes later, the question seems absurd. I am changing whether I wish to or not.

As did you, my love, and I know whose fault that was.

May is the month of growth, of flowering, so now is as good a time as any to begin.

ONE

jfjfjfjfjfjfjfjfjjKDKDKDKDKDKDKDTHE   quick
brown fox;;;;;
=234567890-*)('&—%$#"+
Now
   is
     the
       winter
        of
         our
    It seems to be working. Jim mentioned that there
was an old typewriting machine in one of the upstairs
bedrooms, and I can't resist trying it out. It seems to have
been built in the 1930's by Royal, and it's amazing how
well it works.

This is oddly enjoyable. What should I type?

When I was very young, I thought perhaps I would
be a journalist, so I taught this skill to myself, and that
first paragraph was enough to convince me that it is still

there. I might enjoy sitting here from time to time and putting marks on paper, if I had anything to talk about. To be a journalist, I think, means to have an eye and a memory for detail. Yet my own memory is sufficiently idiosyncratic that I wonder if I would ever have been capable of creating a coherent article, even had my life gone in that direction. The things I remember seem to come in odd gasps, with a picture here, an emotion there, neither in order of importance nor in order chronological, except for the most recent of events.

I recall, for example, from the Christmas party last week, how Mrs. Lockwitt's earring dangled against her neck and reflected light from a fixture of four frosted sixty-watt bulbs. This image is very clear, but things from even a few weeks ago are dim, in that I remember they happened, but could not supply the details.

I remember that Mrs. Lockwitt was saying something to me, but not looking at me as she spoke. I think she said, "There's something foreign about the way you speak," and then turned so that she was facing me. I took the opportunity to observe: slightly round, late forties, heavily powdered. She wore something peach colored that might have looked all right if we weren't in a room where everything was blond wood. I couldn't decide from her remark if she was beginning a conversational gambit or snubbing me, so I gave a brief tight-lipped smile of the sort Miss Manners would have approved of and didn't say anything. She—Mrs. Lockwitt, not Miss Manners—turned back to studying Professor Carpenter's library, filled as it was with books, oak furniture, and academicians in several flavors.

She said, "Have you been around here long?"

I started to say yes, reconsidered, reconsidered again, and said, "A few weeks. Maybe longer or shorter, depending upon what you mean by around here."

There were thirty-five or forty graduate students

and instructors in the house, about half in the library, the others divided between the living room where Miles Davis's *Sketches of Spain* was on the stereo and the kitchen where smoking was allowed. Three or four young students were studying the professor's collection of books, the others were all talking with each other about the breakup of the Eastern Bloc or the imminence of war, or telling jokes that you had to be a third-year student of German literature to understand.

"But you are with the college?" said Mrs. Lockwitt.

I caught her eye, held it, and said, "You don't look like an academic."

"Oh, I'm not," she said, blushing just a little. She was, as I knew already, the professor's lover, and had probably paid for a third of the books in this room, as well as the bust of Voltaire and the Degas that was really very fine work for a print. Carpenter, head of the Modern Languages Department, was a bent stick of a bloodless Englishman, and I wondered how often the two of them had sex, and what it was like. You never know; maybe they made the walls rattle.

I was thinking about leaving. The boring but rather pretty girl named, hmm, whatever her name was, who had invited me to the party had already left, and, more important, I had confirmed what she'd told me—the professor owned a house not far from there which had never been rented. The girl (was it Rachel? Rebecca? something like that) had been trying to convince me of the existence of spirits, and claimed that the house was demon-infested, which is how the subject had come up.

Whether it was or not, I had already pumped Mrs. Lockwitt for the location, and she had confirmed that it was deserted, apparently because she had convinced "Arthur" to move in with her. She said nothing about demons. I don't happen to believe in demons, so I wasn't surprised. I had found what I wanted, though, and was ready to leave. I took a last look around.

Near the door a tall, serious-looking young man wearing a dark sweater and tan knit slacks was engaged in premating rituals with a long-necked beauty in a tight, slinky black dress that came down to her knees and was held up by straps. It wasn't all that flattering, as it made her neck seem even longer, almost deformed. I looked at Mrs. Lockwitt's earring once more, but she didn't seem inclined to continue the conversation. She helped herself from the punch bowl and offered me some. Who puts punch bowls in the library? In any case, I knew what had gone into it, so I declined, excused myself with a gesture, and headed for the probable lovers-to-be.

". . . several generations," he was saying. "All in the same family."

"So you think it's genetic?" she said, sounding more interested than she probably was. "It doesn't surprise me. There are whole families of artists and musicians, why shouldn't mathematics be the same way?"

"Exactly. We're planning a project now with pre-schoolers, testing their aptitudes and relating it to their parents' aptitudes. We're working on a grant proposal with Timson in Biology."

"It sounds exciting," she said, as if trying to convince herself it was. "How far along—" She stopped because I had arrived. They looked at me, holding back their smiles a bit, the way one does with strangers who interrupt a conversation or a mutual seduction. He was half a head taller than I was, and broader; not at all matching the stereotype for people who talk about such things. She was almost my height, but more attractive than I am.

"I don't believe we've met before," I said, shifting my eyes to include them both. "John Agyar. Jack, if you like."

They looked at each other quickly, not knowing how to deal with the interruption. As the silence was becoming uncomfortable, he loosened up a little and said, "Don Swaggart."

"Jill Quarrier."

I looked at her and performed a frown of recognition. "The artist?"

You could practically see her thaw. "You know my work?" I haven't always been good at guesswork, but I've learned.

"I've never had the pleasure of seeing any; but you've been spoken of in very complimentary terms."

"Really? By whom?"

I warmed to her a little; most people would have said "who." "Several people around the department. I don't recall any names, but I was certainly intrigued by what I heard. Do you happen to have anything with you?"

"Yes, do you?" said Young Don, no doubt feeling her attention slip away.

"I'm afraid not," she said, either pleased, disappointed, or both. I couldn't imagine what sort of artist she would be—her face had no animation whatsocvcr. That was all right; it wasn't her face I was interested in.

"Is your work on display at the college?"

"Not at the moment. I have a few pieces at the studio in Berkshire West."

"I'd love to see them."

Donald shifted uncomfortably, probably trying to think of something to say other than "so would I." He settled for asking me, "What department are you with?"

I laughed without showing teeth. "What would you guess?"

She said, "Most people here are Modern Languages, but I'd have guessed you for Drama."

"Really? I think I'm flattered."

Young Don said, "I'd have guessed Business."

I caught his eye and said, "No, I'm afraid not. And you're Sociology."

He frowned. "Good guess."

"No guess," I said. "You fit the profile."

He was wise enough not to ask, but she seemed stung on his behalf and said, "Why is everyone down on sociology? I think the study of how people live together is fascinating."

"People are down on sociology," I said, "because it was invented by people who felt someone ought to answer Marx, and there's no answer for Marx outside of religion, a field any civilized person ought to avoid."

"That's preposterous—" he began.

"What is?"

"Your contention about sociology."

"Oh. I thought you meant my contention about religion."

"What makes you think—"

"Who first popularized the term?"

"Sociology? It was coined by Comte—"

"Who popularized it?"

"I suppose it was Herbert Spencer."

"And what did he say about Marx?"

"Huh? Almost nothing, as a matter of fact."

"And what was the strange thing the dog did in the nighttime?"

Jill laughed, which was half the battle won, and Young Don sputtered, which was the other half. "I don't think you can conclude—"

"Read any Max Weber?" I said.

"Some."

"Well?"

"Are you a Marxist?" He probably thought it was a good counterattack, but I couldn't help laughing, both at the question and at his predicament.

"Not likely," I said. "Merely a student of applied realities. And a lover of art. And a cardplayer."

Donny frowned as the conversation went completely out of his reckoning. "You're a gambler?"

"Not when I can help it," I said. "You?"

"Uh, no."

It was time to bring Jill back into it. "How about you?"

She gave the question more consideration than it was worth; probably the overintellectual type. "Sometimes," she said. "Gambling can be exciting."

"Winning is better, if you know how."

"You know how?" she said, trying to act a little amused.

"Yes."

"Tell me."

"Show me your paintings, and I'll let you in on the secret."

"Sure," she said, laughing. "When?"

"Now," I said. "Unless you're finding the party too exciting to slip away from."

"You have wheels?"

"No, I have feet. It's a lovely night, and Berkshire isn't far."

"It's cold."

"Not too cold; there's no wind."

She looked up at me through squinted eyes. Her brows were fair and I saw the faint blond roots of her dark hair. Amusing. Our eyes locked for a moment, and I thought I detected a sense of humor down there somewhere, as if she knew what was was happening and thought it was funny. Maybe she thought she was gambling. In any case, Young Don was forgotten. "All right," she said. We went to the hallway, where I helped her with her parka of some synthetic material. My coat was the authentic English bobby's coat; very natty. Stylish. We left together, while Donald was carefully looking in another direction.

The night was the cold of Midwestern mid-winter with a big moon, a day shy of full, but mostly hidden by high, fast clouds. There were few streetlights. No one was out, save a howling dog a block away, an owl who darted from tree to tree in a vain search for winter rodents, three rats whom the owl didn't notice, and one dark gray cat who kept appearing, staring at us, then vanishing behind the houses. The rats smelled like the sewers they lived in; I was pleased when we were past them. Eventually the cat left us alone, at around the same time the dog stopped howling. Either the dog's master had shut it up, or the cat had killed it. Fine either way.

I offered her my arm and she took it. "What's the secret, Jack?" she said.

"Always keep a few important cards where no one can see them."

"That's it? Cheat?"

"You call that cheating?"

"Don't you?"

"Where do you live?"

"Off-campus housing. On Fullbright. A big, white house with blue lights coming out of the attic."

"Do you live in the attic?"

"No. Are you really a gambler?"

"As I said, not when I can help it."

"All right, then, a cardplayer?"

"I enjoy card games."

"For money?"

"Sometimes."

"Is that how you make your living?"

I laughed at that, but didn't explain why. Her touch on my arm sent the message that she might be getting annoyed, but by then we were practically at Berkshire. She had a key so she opened the door and went inside. I studied the mid-nineteenth century archway. She said, "What are you waiting for?"

"I'm trying to figure out whose work this is."

"Oh. You're into architecture?"

"Not really," I said.

She looked puzzled and held the door open for me. I entered, and she led me down to the studio to show me her etchings. *Finis.*

I stopped typing a few hours ago, took the last page out of the machine, and set it facedown on the pile to my left, as if I had finished and wouldn't resume. I've spent the intervening time sitting here, staring into space. I suppose I might as well keep typing.

This room, the one with the typewriting machine, seems to have been redone in the 1950's, then partly redone again in the late seventies, probably just before the house was abandoned. There used to be wallpaper, but now there is bare plasterboard thick with splotches of greenish glue. The windows are boarded shut, and I type by the light of a single candle, one of those thick tall ones that can stand on its own without a holder. It has been scented with what someone thought was apple blossom, and I suppose it is closer to that than anything else, but it isn't very close, nor is it strong. I can still smell the wood as it collects pockets of moisture and rots. The desk drawers, still full of desk things, are heaped next to me, as if when Professor Carpenter moved away he wanted to take it with him, then changed his mind, not thinking the desk worth the trouble. I guess he was right; it is small and cheaply built of plywood. I wonder why he left the typing machine, though. One of the desk drawers contains most of a ream of paper, however; good enough paper to have survived these ten or fifteen years.

I am pleased at how well my skill at working this machine has returned. The sound of the type bars striking the paper and the little rattle of the keys do not echo, perhaps because of the textured ceiling. There are still a few mice in the walls; I wonder what they live on.

What else to talk about?

I suppose I could continue where I left off a few hours ago, and bring matters up to the point where they stand now.

I left Jill sleeping deeply on the cot in her studio, went back to the train depot, and the next day went and looked at the house. The neighborhood is quiet, not too well lit, and situated not far from Twain. I decided it would do, so I made the arrangements to have my things moved.

Bah. I don't want to talk about all of that. It was more than a week ago, and old news is dull, even when writing to one's self. What about last night? That's more interesting, because I've finally heard from Kellem.

I spent all night looking for a place to play cards without finding one. When I finally gave up, I made my way to this place that is home for here and now. I threw my coat over the end table next to the window, closed the window against the increasing chill, and opened the front door. There was a small slip of paper in the mailbox. It was in Gaelic for some reason, and said, "Day after tomorrow, 10:30, outside Howard's—L." I went back inside, burned the note in the fireplace, and stretched out in what was left of a bulky stuffed gray chair that someone had decided wasn't worth moving. The springs on one side of it were broken, so I sat with a list to starboard.

These tenses are interesting. I don't know whether to write, "the springs were broken," because they were when I was sitting on it, or, "the springs are broken," because as I sit here they still are. The first way is somehow more entertaining, like I'm telling myself a nice little story, but it also seems contrived. Funny, the things you never think about until you set about committing them to the page.

For that matter, I hadn't given much thought to Laura Kellem, although she is the reason I've come to this little star in the map next to Lake Erie. Even now, when I think of her, all I get are moments, ripped out of time, with emotional harmonics but no melody for context. I can close my eyes and see her, looking at me with an expression that, at the time, I took for tenderness, but that I later came to believe was only a vague cousin—the fondness one might feel for a cat who lived with a close friend.

Odd, that. How long has it been since I have had a close friend? Will I ever again? Perhaps. Jim and I seem to be hitting it off rather well, I suppose because neither of us has anything the other wants. Which, now that I think of it, was never true of Laura and I, even when we were close—or what passed for close between us.

It was close on my part, I think. I cared for her. I'd have to say that I loved her, with the sort of burning passion that I then knew how to feel, and now know how to inspire. It would probably be trite to say, "What goes around comes around," but that's what it feels like.

I remember how I felt, though, when she would escort me through Vienna or Paris. I can still recall the pressure of her hand on my arm. To this day, I don't know how much affection she felt for me and how much she just found it amusing to have me so infatuated with her. I certainly can't ask her. And I'm not even sure I want to find out.

And yet I know that she is capable of intense feelings, or, at any rate, she was once. I remember sitting in a cafe in, well, somewhere where they had cafes. It was closed, and the streets were deserted, but we were sitting there nevertheless, and she started telling me about a man named Broadwin or something like that. Her eyes became soft, almost misty, and she said, "He had such big hands, Jack. When he held me he was all the world. I'd look up into his face and see nothing but his eyes looking down at me."

"Where is he now?" I asked casually, because I felt the stirrings of something like jealousy.

"He's dead," she told me. "Years later, he became involved with some bit of fluff in Scotland, and lost his head. Figuratively, at first." Then her voice changed and she came back to the present. "Take that as a lesson, Agyar János."

"I will," I told her. And I did, too. A couple of lessons, in fact. One of them is that, at one time in her life, she felt something. I wonder if it could ever happen again? Probably not.

But where was I? Right. I was sitting in the chair, just at the point when Jim the ghost came noiselessly down the stairs and stood translucently in front of me, nearly six feet tall, well dressed, black, with a round face, thick neck, broad shoulders, and very short white hair. He was dressed, as ever, in his funereal best; white shirt and string tie. "You look disgruntled," he said.

"This is a boring city."

"Maybe. You seemed to like the party last week."

"It wasn't bad. For a college party. I was surprised at the number of disciplines in attendance."

"That's a trademark of Artie. What did you think of him, by the way?"

"Artie? Professor Carpenter?"

"Yes."

"Never really had the chance to talk to him. His mistress let me in. Why?"

"His grandfather was one of my instructors."

"Is that how you know him?"

"No, he used to live here."

"Oh. That's right. Why did he leave?"

"He began to think the place was haunted."

"Oh," I said. And, "He has an ugly mistress."

Jim laughed and looked at the pendant I wear on my chest, which is a large chunk of black petrified wood, polished and set in silver. He was only looking at it because he never looked anyone in the eyes, I suspect even when he was alive. Since I'm an eye-contact person, that always makes conversations with him a little uncomfortable. It was also a little disturbing to see the black vertical line of the fireplace poker through his clothing, as if it were a decoration on his trousers. I should imagine that I'll become used to this sort of thing, if I remain here for any length of time.

Which subject, in fact, Jim brought up sometime while we were talking. "Do you know how long you'll be staying?" he said.

"You mean in Lakota? Or in this house."

"Well, both."

"Am I bothering you?"

"Au contraire. I like the company."

"Au contraire?" I said. "What is this *au* god damn *contraire?"*

He winced just a little at the profanity and said, "You forget that I's a eddicated nigguh."

"Right. I don't know how long I'll be around. Word reached me that an acquaintance was here and wanted to see me. I'll see what she wants, then be on my way. I prefer bigger cities, in general."

"Why are you going to her rather than the other way around?"

"She's older than me."

"So?"

"You ask too many questions."

"What are you going to do, kill me?"

I laughed. "Where and what is Howard's?" I said.

"I don't know; find a phone book."

"Good idea," I said. "Do you have paper and pens here, in case I want to write to her?"

"Better than that, there's a typewriter in one of the upstairs rooms. Can you type?"

"I used to. I'll take a look at it tomorrow. There's paper?"

"Yes."

"Good," I said, then yawned.

"Tired?"

"Yes. It's winter. I always get more tired in winter."

"Seems reasonable. Shall I light the way, suh?"

"With what?"

"Mah two glowin' eyes."

"Don't bother. Just practice up the poltergeist stuff in case anyone tries to wake me."

"Shore, bawse."

"Thanks. I'll double your salary."

He probably would have said "Shit," but, as I had already learned, Jim never, ever swore. I went down to my room and slept.

Here it is, less than forty-eight hours since I left this machine, and I'm back here again, though I'm not certain why.

It is always strange to be in the grip of emotion and not know what that emotion is. Or, to put it another way, to have been through the sort of experience that ought to engender a strong response, to be waiting to feel that response. I'm not sure if I want to set it down at all, yet I feel the need to tap on these keys. It's addicting, I think, this business of putting one word after another. Byron mentioned something about that once while he was sick from taking too much of some drug or another.

I got up several hours before the appointed hour, so I showered, brushed my teeth (the house, though deserted, has its own well, the pump of which still works), got dressed, then found a flower shop just as it was closing. The proprietor took pity and invited me in, and I ordered a bunch of purple roses to be sent to Jill. I toyed with having a cactus sent to young Don, and I might have done so if I'd known how to reach him.

I took a turn around part of the city, getting to know it the way as a young man I'd gotten to know the twists and turns and buildings at University. I listened in on a few private conversations, just because they were there, but heard nothing worth the trouble of repeating. Eventually I found a phone booth. The difference between Lakota and Staten Island can be expressed in the fact that the phone booth had a city directory in it, looking as if there was no reason for it not to be there. I looked up the address of Howard's, asked directions of a young man getting into a blue '86 Ford Pinto, and set out for Woodwright Avenue, called the Ave, which was in the sort of funky part of town, called the Tunnel, that lies between two of the colleges.

Howard's turned out to be a nightclub on the Ave with a fake wood front and a covered entryway complete with doorman and red carpet, just like in a real city. I think it is what they call "trendy." A useful word. Whenever the door opened I could hear nonthreatening jazz creep hesitantly out onto the street, then change its mind and slink back inside when the door closed. To my eyes, Kellem blended into the scene the way Bette Midler would have blended into a monastery, yet no one seemed to notice her.

It's funny how I'd forgotten so much of what she looked like. She is about five feet ten inches tall, has red hair and the pale complexion that goes with it. Her face is thin, with strong bones and very bright blue eyes. She had a thin red scarf wrapped around her throat. Her camel-colored coat was thick, elegant, and short. Beneath it she wore dark trousers and low boots. What I noticed right away, however, was that she had a few bald patches on top of her head. I couldn't imagine what would cause that, but I made up my mind not to ask unless she brought it up. In any case, the patrons didn't notice either one of us much.

She saw me at about the same time I saw her, and walked up to meet me. "Agyar," she said.

"Kellem."

"How long have you been in town?"

"A little more than a month."

"Really? It took you a while to find a place?"

"Yes. I didn't know you were in a hurry."

"I'm not. But you're settled in now?"

"Pretty well."

"Good. Hungry?"

"No. You?"

"Always." She smiled without humor. "But let's just walk and talk."

"Sure. Your place?"

"Funny, Agyar.

"You know where I live."

"That's different, as you well know."

I shrugged. "Lead on, then."

She did, taking us a block away from the Ave, onto a side street called Drewry where there was no traffic and most of the houses already had their lights out. Someone once told me it never really got cold in Northeastern Ohio, but either that someone lied or he was Canadian. A pair of squirrels woke up as we walked by their tree, then went back to sleep. Mama raccoon ducked back into her sewer. She smelled like the rats had.

"Any trouble finding a place to stay?" asked Laura.

I shrugged. "As I said, I took my time. There was no problem keeping everything locked up in the train depot."

"How did you come across the house?"

"I just walked around and listened to gossip. I heard about Carpenter deserting a house, tracked him down, got invited to a party, found out where the house was, and moved my things in. I had no trouble gaining entry, because no one lived there. So to speak."

She chuckled. "Does Carpenter know?"

"No."

"Well, thanks for coming so quickly."

"I had nothing pressing. What's on your mind?"

"Settling down."

"Not a bad idea. I've done it myself, once or twice."

"Do you believe in omens?"

"Does the Pope believe in bears?"

"What about dreams?"

"Dreams. I'm not certain about dreams. Why?"

"I've been having some odd ones."

"What about?"

"Children. That is, my own."

"Have you any?"

"Not in the conventional sense."

"And that's the sort you've been dreaming of?"

"Yes."

"And it seems significant?"

"Very."

"In what way?"

"I'm not going to live forever, you know."

"An axiom, Kellem, without substance."

"Maybe, but that's not how it's been feeling."

"Is that why you've brought me out here? Because you've been having dreams?"

"I brought you out here because I knew how to reach you, and I needed to reach someone."

"To talk about your dreams?"

"Not exactly."

"Well?"

There were a pair of kids, a boy and a girl, both

about seventeen, across the street talking about what they were going to do when the year ended. She'd go to school in town, probably at Twain, and he was going to apply to MIT in Boston. The calendar year would be ending in another few weeks, but I decided they probably meant the school year. That was all right, one is as arbitrary as the other, and the year as measured by the progression of seasons doesn't really mean anything in a city. Their conversation faded into the background din of man and nature, who keep changing each other and making noise while doing so.

"The dreams have been affecting me," she said. "I've done some strange things."

"Taken chances?"

"All of that."

"What sort of chances?"

"The sort you take when you're desperate, and not really in control of your actions."

"Can you be more specific?"

"I'm not sure."

"If you want help, you must tell Doctor Agyar—"

"Cut it out."

I spread my hands, palms up, and waited. When she didn't continue I said, "Do you think someone might have noticed?"

"Yes," she said in a neutral tone, so I couldn't tell if she was worried, angry, or only vaguely interested.

"Can you cut and run?"

"I don't want to."

"Why?"

"I like it here."

I looked around elaborately. The streets were lined with trees, mostly oak and sycamore. The houses were working-class one-family dwellings, this one blue, that one yellow, that one green, with nothing to choose among them except lawn ornaments.

"You don't understand," she said.

"No."

"I go into coffee shops and talk with artists who are actually creating something. I go to plays, or movie theaters, and meet people with children who talk about how little Johnny speaks in full sentences and he's only two years old. I—"

"And you like it?"

"Yes."

"And now and then you do a convenience store or a bank."

"When I'm desperate for cash; not often."

"And lately you've been committing indiscretions."

"That's right. I think I have it under control now, though."

"That's good. Then what do you want me for?"

She looked me in the eyes for the first time. Hers were blue, large, and very, very cold. "As I said, the indiscretions have been noticed."

"So what do you want me for?"

"Someone has to take the fall," she said. "It's going to be you."

The night whispered around us, alive but indifferent.

TWO

or·gan·ic *adj.* . . . 2. Of, pertaining to, or derived from living organisms . . . 4. Having properties associated with living organisms . . . 6. a. Of or constituting an integral part of something; fundamental; constitutional; structural.

AMERICAN HERITAGE DICTIONARY

I keep discovering ways in which age affects me. For example, when I was younger and, as I said before, considering a career in journalism, I tried to keep a diary, because this had been recommended to me by a professor at University as a way of training myself, but I could never do it. Yet now I find that, as I go through my day, my thoughts keep coming back to this old typewriting machine and I eagerly await the chance to return to it. I don't understand the reason for this change, and I haven't the patience for soul-searching.

I don't think, though, that it is really the need to set down what happens, as much as it is the act of writing, or typing, itself. There is something soothing in hearing the type bars smack the paper with that hollow, crunching sound, and seeing the black marks appear. They are nice and black, because I found a new ribbon in one of the desk drawers that sits next to this hard wooden chair, and after considerable trouble I managed to get it threaded the right way. Then I had to go wash the ink off my hands, because it seems wrong to soil the keys of this venerable machine.

Yesterday I rushed home after meeting with Kellem and, before anything else, I set it all down as well as I could. The act of doing so was very soothing, more so, it turned out, than telling it all to Jim the ghost, which I did as soon as I was done typing. Yet there were things, important things, that I didn't remember as I typed them. Some of these came back, however, as I told Jim about the conversation. Why is it that some memories cast themselves naturally into written words, while others must be spoken?

As Jim and I conversed, he played with an old nickel, hole punched in the center, with a thin chain running through the hole. When I had finished, he put it around his neck, under his shirt, and looked at me. He said, "Did she give you any details about what she'd done that you're supposed to suffer for?"

"There have been some bodies, apparently."

"Just bodies?"

"What more do you want, zombies?"

"Never seen a zombie."

"Never hope to see one. But I can tell you, Abercrombie—"

"Not sure I believe in zombies," said Jim.

"Nor am I. But no, just bodies."

"What about witnesses?"

"She's no fool."

"Then why does she need someone to go down for the killings?"

"She wants the investigations settled before the authorities dig something up, as it were."

"Why you?"

"I suppose because I'll confess to them, and that will end it."

He stared past my shoulder, his eyes wide as the moon and looming like a stereotype. "Why will you do that?"

"Because she told me to."

"And there's nothing you can do about it?"

"No. Orders, as they say, are orders."

"I don't understand."

"You know what they say about Hell hath no fury and all that."

"You scorned her?"

"No, actually, she scorned me, if you want to look at it that way."

"I don't understand."

"If you love someone who doesn't love you, you're in her power, and power is what this is all about. With Kellem, power is always what it is about."

"And you still love her?"

"No."

"Then—"

"It's complicated, Jim."

He shook his head, still confused. There was no good way to explain it, so I didn't. He said, "When will it happen?"

"I don't know. I imagine she hasn't worked out all the details. It could be tricky for her. I am, as you might guess, overwhelmed with sympathy for her."

The wind whistled merrily through the wooden slats over the windows on the north side of the house, facing the border of honeysuckle bushes, which are as tall as a man; they died in last year's drought, but have not yet fallen. Soon they will fall apart, I think, and the wind will whistle merrier still. A cheery place, this old house where Jim the ghost has given me temporary residence.

After a while, Jim said, "I can't believe there's nothing you can do."

"Let's talk about it outside."

"You know I can't—oh."

I stretched out into the chair and looked at the yellowed ceiling, where shadows from the candle flickered and danced. Jim stood there. I wish he'd sit down sometimes, but I don't imagine his legs get tired.

"Thing is," he said a little later, "you sound like you don't care."

"Don't care? No, it's not that. I don't want to die, I suppose, but—"

"You suppose?"

"What's the point of worrying about it? There's nothing I can do. I mean, I imagine, given a choice, I'd like to go on living, but—"

"You imagine?"

I didn't answer for a moment. Jim watched me, or at least my chest, without saying anything.

"Should I start a fire?" I said.

"That would be pleasant," said Jim. "I'm not certain the flue works, however."

"I'll check into it," I said.

"What if someone sees the smoke?"

"There shouldn't be much if the wood is dry, and there are only a couple of houses across the street. Besides, this area isn't lighted as well as some."

The flue was not seriously clogged. I brought some old, rotting firewood in from the old, rotting carriage house, found some newspapers in a neighbor's trash can, and lit the fire from one of the candles.

"Won't burn long with those old logs," said Jim.

"It's getting late anyway," I said, stifling a yawn and watching the thickly curling smoke that old bark produces.

"A fire like this wants hot spiced brandy, or cider, or even tea."

"If you make it," I said, "I'll drink it."

"Don't have any," said Jim.

"Me neither."

A few sparks shot up the chimney and out to defy the winter.

It has been several days now since I felt like coming up here, I guess because there isn't much satisfaction in talking about how I shower, eat, read the newspapers, and sleep. It's only when I meet someone and we affect each other that I feel I have anything to write down.

I went back to visit Jill earlier tonight, this time at her house. It would have been harder to find if she hadn't mentioned the blue light in the attic, but there it was, and there I was. The place had just been painted, sometime within the last couple of months; the smell had survived the weather and it overpowered any other smells. I've never been fond of paint smell, but there are worse. I heard sounds of a stereo faintly through the door and recognized 3 Mustaphas 3; it's always interesting when you discover someone who knows the same obscure music you know. There's very little contemporary music of any kind that I listen to, and when I discover a musician I like it is usually by accident. In this case, I dated a woman in New York who worked for a record company, and several times found myself waiting for her in her offices, and they were played there. I know the songs they play, and they have more respect for the music than most.

I shouldn't let myself get started on this, should I?

But I did, in fact, like the music, and I wondered if I'd misjudged Jill. Probably not. I stood on a very wide, very long unenclosed porch, with a few pieces of cheap furniture. The door was thick and wooden, with no screen. I looked for a buzzer and didn't find one. Knock knock went the nice man at the door.

The music dropped in volume to the point where I could hear the slap of bare feet against a wood floor. The door opened with a melodramatic creak, and two very wide blue eyes appeared vertically in the partially opened doorway. No, it wasn't Jill. I couldn't see the smile below the eyes, but the lines around the cheekbones indicated it was there.

"Yes?" she said. "And who might you be?"

I bowed, because it seemed the appropriate response. "I might be Jill's friend," I said. "Or I might be an Israeli terrorist looking for PLO supporters. Or possibly a burglar trying to steal your jewels to support my laudanum habit. Or even a neighbor complaining about the volume. That is "Heart of Uncle," isn't it? It really ought to be louder."

She considered this, worked her lips like Nero Wolfe, then threw the door open all the way, placed her hand against the doorjamb while leaning against the casing trim. She had one leg bent, her foot resting against the doorway, and her arms were folded in front of her as she blocked the doorway and considered me. She was as tall as I and thinner; most of her height in her legs. She wore a navy blue skirt, buttoned on the side, and a white tank top. She was small-breasted, with a graceful neck and a delightfully animated face, full of blue eyes and theatrical expressions. Her hair was dark blond, straight, and reached only to the top of her neck, with a navy blue band keeping it back out of her face. Her lips were full and had just a hint of a cupid's bow. Her nose was small, and she probably wrinkled it fairly often, for effect. I decided she couldn't possibly be a drama student because stereotypes are never that perfect.

"I like your coat," she announced, as if her approval of my dress were the supreme prize in a good-taste contest.

"Does that mean I get to see Jill?"

She considered this. "Perhaps it does," she said.

"Just what are your intentions concerning my room-mate?"

"I'm going to kidnap her and hold her for ransom."

"Really?" she said, appearing delighted. "How splendid."

"Or else I'll put her in a cage and show her for money, but I think you'd be more suitable for that role."

She nodded. "Yes. The kidnapping is a much better idea." She stood straight and walked with exaggerated grace into the living room. There was a very nice wooden stairway, curving back on itself with a stained-glass window at the landing. She called, "Jill! Your kidnapper is here," and gave me a big smile.

"Aren't you going to come in?" she said.

"Only if you want me to. We kidnappers are very polite."

"Oh do, by all means."

"My name is Jack Agyar."

"I am Susan," she said, giving me an elaborate curtsy. "Susan Pfahl." I left my Wellingtons in the entry-way and passed inside. There was a very nice ceiling fixture, with old, presumably dead, gas jets mixed into the more modern decorative lamps. They cast downward-pointing sharp shadows against the printed white wallpaper. The pattern was of roses, but nicely subdued. The furnishings didn't all match each other, but all went with the polished maple floor, the high, smooth white ceiling, and the dark wood of the stairway and around the fireplace.

"Dance or music?" I said.

"Both," she said, smiling. "Would you like to hear me sing?"

"Yes."

She sang, "Laaaaaaaa," at a high pitch, filling up the room, her arms spread as if she were finishing a solo at the Met.

I said, "Hire the kid."

Jill called from the stairs, "My god, Susan, don't break the glasses."

"I shan't," she said.

Jill wore faded jeans, a plaid work shirt, and pale yellow deck shoes. I looked quickly back and forth and wondered if it was too late to change my mind. I smiled at Jill and said, "How are you on this fine evening?"

"Okay," she said. "I'm surprised to see you."

"Not unpleasantly I hope."

She made a vague gesture and said, "What's up?"

"I thought I might take you out."

"Hmmm. I sort of have to study."

"Let's talk about it. Upstairs." I didn't quite leer.

She glanced at Susan, blushed, started to say something, decided to get angry, changed her mind, and said, "All right," in a very low voice. She went upstairs and I followed.

Her room was done in light blue, with a twin bed against the wall, head near the window, a green stuffed turtle on the flower-patterned comforter and a single white pillow. There were a couple of prints of abstract art on the wall, one of red lines and watery pastels, the other seemed to be a meaningless pattern of black needles against a green background. I'm sure they were both meaningful. In one corner were a few small canvases, and from the two I could see they were clearly her work, judging by the lack of style. Her desk sat in a corner and held a Webster's Collegiate dictionary, an ashtray with a few marijuana buds, a round copper incense holder, a picture of her that I guessed to have been taken by a bored family photographer when she was about sixteen, a coffee mug full of pens and pencils, an electric typing machine, and a pad of drawing paper.

She said, "Don't embarrass me in front of Susan."

"Why were you embarrassed?"

"Just don't, all right?"

I smiled into her eyes. "Give us a kiss, then," I said.

She sighed and came into my arms. I caressed her back for a moment, and held her cheek against mine. Her skin was warm and soft. I kissed my way past her ear.

"Jack," she said in a whisper.

"Hmmm?"

"I don't—"

"I do, however, and that's what matters."

She came around to my way of thinking in pretty short order. When I went back down the stairs Susan was still up, stretched out like a cat on the sofa, her ankles crossed. Something I didn't recognize was on the stereo. She seemed to be listening intently, although she must have heard me come down, because she opened one eye and said, "That was quick."

"Jill was mad at me," I said. "It seems I embarrassed her."

"Jill," said Susan, "embarrasses easily."

"You don't though," I said.

"That is correct."

"Then I won't try to embarrass you. Grab a coat."

"Where are we going?"

"Coffee."

She smiled a very nice smile and said, "I'd like that."

I had draped my coat over a chair. I retrieved it, and she was ready by the time I had my Wellies on. Her coat was green wool, double-breasted, belted, and knee length, with a large collar. She wore no hat. "I shall not bring my purse," she said, "since this is your treat."

"Exactly."

She didn't lock the door on the way out. She took my arm at once and said, "I don't believe I shall call you Jack."

"No? What will you call me?"

"I don't know. John isn't right, either."

"Perhaps Jonathan."

"Hmmm. Jonathan. Yes, that might do. Come here, Jonathan. Yes." She repeated it a couple of times, and I guess decided it would do. She looked at me and smiled. Her mouth was large, her jaw line prominent.

I said, "I hope Jill won't be angry with you."

"Gillian," she said, "must learn to look out for her territory."

"You mean that in general?"

"Yes."

"Explain."

"When we moved in together, I told her that I would be claiming as much of the house as I could until she stopped me, so she had better be prepared to defend her turf or I'd simply take over."

"And she hasn't done so?"

"You saw the house; did it look like her or me?"

"What makes you think I can tell the difference?"

"You can tell."

I laughed. "You," I said.

"Correct."

"The attitude," I said, "seems ever so slightly harsh."

"Do you think so?" she inquired sweetly. "Maybe it is, but I don't have the patience to put up with having to ask every time I want to move a piece of furniture or put a new vase on the mantelpiece."

"So you just do it?"

"She can tell me if she doesn't like it."

"And she's never said anything?"

"No."

"Then it's her problem."

"Exactly."

"And do I fall into the same category?"

She smiled brightly. "Yes."

"Nice to know where I fit in."

"Where do you fit in?" she said.

"Do you mean that philosophically or practically?"

"Either way."

"I'm more or less just passing through, so I guess I really don't fit in."

"Do you mean that philosophically or practically?"

"Either way. Did Jill say anything about me?"

Susan looked at me through slitted eyes, as if deciding how much to tell. At last she said, "Jill seemed quite taken with you at first, especially when you sent her flowers."

"At first?"

"Well, it's been, what, a week? And you haven't called."

"Has it been a week already? How time flies. Well, has she waited for me, breathlessly, anxiously, sitting by the phone and staring out the window?"

Susan laughed. "Hardly."

I pretended dismay. "Don't tell me she has another man already?"

"I'm not certain." She smiled wickedly. "Well, there is this gentleman who's called on her a couple of times in the last week."

"Ah!" I said. "A rival! Who is he?"

"His name is Don something."

"Swaggart? The sociologist? She's been seeing him?"

"As I said, just once or twice. Does that bother you?"

"I am beside myself with jealousy."

She laughed again. "I can tell."

"How well do you know the dear boy?"

She made a noncommittal gesture. "Well enough to know that there's not a lot of substance to him."

"But," I said, "he's very dedicated to his work."

"Is he?"

We walked a little more. We occasionally passed people. She said, "That's what you get for not striking while the iron is hot."

"That's what she gets for being impatient. Let it be a lesson to you."

"Oh, she's not nearly as impatient as I am. Once I got so annoyed waiting for my bus, that I got on the next one that came by, just to be going somewhere."

I laughed.

She said, "Are you going to do anything about Don?"

"What do you propose I do?"

"I was just wondering."

"To be perfectly frank, I don't much care one way or the other," I said.

We arrived at an all-night coffee place called the Wholly Ground. There didn't seem to be anyone in it. I stood in the doorway and asked if they were open, but Susan breezed in. A poster outside advertised the appearance of something called the Beat Farmers, but the place didn't seem to have a stage. I had just noticed that the poster was for somewhere else when Susan motioned me in. "They're open all night," she said, at the same time as the short-haired nose-ringed girl behind the counter nodded. It was a small place that smelled harshly of coffee and rank tobacco smoke. All the tables were round and most had room for four coffee cups and an ashtray; you had to hold your morning paper.

I bought us a pot of coffee for three dollars while Susan fetched cups. "Do you use cream?" she said.

"Black like my heart."

She smiled all over her face and said, "How wonderful. I believe we shall get along splendidly."

We sat near a window where we could watch passersby. I filled her cup, left mine half empty. Or half full, if you want to join the Peace Corps. She looked a question. "Keeps me awake," I said.

"They serve unleaded."

"Never touch the stuff."

I brought the cup to my lips. "It also cools faster this way."

"You don't like it hot?"

"Lukewarm like my heart," I said.

She laughed. Her laugh was merry and seemed contrived like her speech and other mannerisms; yet, like her speech and mannerisms, not unpleasantly so.

"Tell me about the city," I said.

"It is a city like other cities," she said at once. "Only not so big."

"How big is it?"

"Less than half a million people, and not very spread out."

"What do people do here?"

"Live. Die. Breed."

"Sing? Dance?"

"Music is life, and life is dance, as Vivian used to say."

"Who's Vivian?"

"A friend."

"Where are you from?"

"New York, New York," she sang.

"I just came from there."

"Where?"

"I was living on Staten Island for a while."

"And before that?"

"Ah, my dear, London, Paris, Istanbul, Tokyo."

"Tokyo? Really?"

"I didn't like it."

"Why not?"

"I don't speak Japanese."

"Oh. Yes, that would be a problem. What languages do you speak?"

"The language of love. And you?"

"The language of dance, of song. Tra-la, tra-la."

"But are you understood?"

"Sometimes I am. Are you?"

"Oh, my, yes. Always."

"I believe that, Jonathan."

I poured her some more coffee, warmed mine up a bit. I stared out the window. "Is winter fog usual around here?"

"It happens," she said. "But there isn't any fog tonight."

"No, but there will be."

"Do you think so? I like the fog."

"And thunderstorms."

"Yes. Especially thunderstorms. They're my favorite part of living in the Midwest; that and the clouds. How do you know there will be fog tonight?"

"It has that feel."

"Jonathan, do you ever get the feeling you know what's going to happen?"

"Sometimes. You?"

"Yes."

"So tell me, what do you think is going to happen?"

She grinned and cocked her head to the side. "Why, I think we're going to have a winter fog."

We did, too, but that was several hours later, after I had escorted her home, and left her at the door after kissing her hand in my most courtly fashion. Most amateurs at hand-kissing make it a bow, with eyes down. Properly, you should be looking at your intended the entire time, with an expression at once tender and slightly amused. The kiss ought to be a single touch of the lips, neither too short nor too long; the actual caress is carried out by your hand squeezing hers—and oh, so delicately, so she isn't quite certain if you have caressed her or not.

I left her at her door, enjoying the tension between our conversation, clearly aimed at the bedroom, and our physical contact, which had been limited to her hand on my arm, and one kiss of her hand. I had intended to poke my head in and look in on Jill, who hadn't been feeling entirely well when I left her, but I could hardly spoil a gesture like that, so I just turned around and left.

By that time there was, indeed, a fog rolling in, which became thicker as I made my way back to Professor Carpenter's house. There was no moon whatsoever, both because it was new and because it had already set. It was about two-thirty in the morning and Lakota was, if not buried, at least pretty dead. I had no trouble finding the place, even in the fog, and since I was certain no one could see me, I took the opportunity to enter, if not break in.

Two people, a small dog, and a cat were breathing quietly in the house. I had not noticed the cat the first time I was there. Perhaps she was shy.

I had no reason to disturb any of them, so I moved quietly and tested my hypothesis that a professor who owned a large house would not put his desk in the same room he slept in. It didn't seem like a particularly daring guess, and it turned out to be right. My second hypothesis was that his address book would be in plain sight on said desk. This was more daring and turned out not to be the case. Neither was it in any of the desk drawers, but rather, for some reason, it turned out to be on a bookshelf. I scanned through it quickly, found what I wanted, memorized it, then took myself out the way I came. The dog never even woke up.

On the other hand, there was still the question: Now that I had the address, what, if anything, was I going to do with it? I thought about Laura Kellem, and consequences, and tried to decide if I cared. I wasn't certain.

But then I considered the significance of what Susan had told me, and I wasn't certain I cared about that, either.

There were no lights on when I got home, but I hadn't expected any.

THREE

suf·fer *v.—intr.* 1. To feel pain or distress; sustain loss, injury, harm, or punishment. 2. To tolerate or endure evil, injury, pain, or death. 3. To appear at a disadvantage. —*tr.* . . . 2. To experience . . . 4. To permit; allow. . . .

AMERICAN HERITAGE DICTIONARY

It's funny; when I finished my last session of typing I realized I was disappointed that there was no more to relate, and I went on down to find Jim, with the idea clearly in mind of getting him talking so I could come back to this machine and set it all down. I've been challenging myself to see how much of a conversation I could actually remember, and I suppose at heart I'm a liar, because ever since I started I've been willing to fabricate conversations that I could have summarized easily and accurately. I don't know why it is more satisfying to see those inverted commas that Joyce hated so passionately, even if I can only remember the essence of what was said.

On the other hand, it feels as if I'm getting better at remembering exact quotations. This may be imagination at work.

But I did go downstairs, and Jim was standing, his arms clasped behind him, staring at the dead fireplace. I said, "Jim, what do you *do* around here?"

He turned his head so he was almost looking at me over his shoulder. "You mean, to earn my keep?"

"No, I mean to kill time. Being a ghost seems like the most wearying thing I can think of."

"Have you ever studied Latin?"

"Okay, the second most wearying."

He shook his head. "I don't do anything, but I'm not bored."

"I don't understand."

"It's never boring to be what you are. It's not usually exciting either. You just exist."

"That's what most people do most of the time. That's what I mean by wearying."

"And what do you do?"

"At least I have some contact with other people."

"And I don't?"

"Do you?"

"If I didn't, this house wouldn't be deserted."

"Well, but since then?"

"I watch people go by, I listen to the wind. I've followed two generations of owls who live on top of the carriage house. And I reminisce."

"On your life?"

He nodded, staring past my shoulder. His eyes weren't focused.

I said, "How did you get educated? There weren't black colleges then, were there?"

"No, I had to go to white folks' school. They thought it was funny to see me there, but it wasn't unheard of, the way it was later."

"But how did it happen?"

"I had a friend who had money. I think he thought it would be funny if his friend the nigger had a college education." He didn't sound bitter when he said it; he didn't sound much of anything.

"I'll bet you spoke differently then."

"Yes."

"Want to give me a demonstration? I'm curious."

"No."

"It *was* after the Civil War, wasn't it?"

"Yeah, but I was already free before the war."

"Given your freedom, or did you escape?"

"Both. It's a long story."

"I have time."

"I don't have the inclination." Suddenly, then, he looked directly at me for the first time. He said, "I *did* run away, though. No one can hold you if you don't want to be held."

"Heh."

He looked away again. "You better believe it. I lived through things that—I lived through things. And I went to a university. And I learned that you can't hold a man who doesn't want to be held."

"How did you die, anyway?"

He twitched a little, like something had bitten him. Then he smiled. "Touché," he said, which was the only answer I got out of him.

Bah.

Enough of this.

My latest discovery is that too much sitting in one place and recording what has gone on is frustrating; it makes me wish to go out and do something. I am, by nature, unaccustomed to inaction; I think I must be a sort of counterpoint to Jim, the way t'ai chi is the counterpoint to meditation. This may be a poor example, all I know of either one is what I learned from a young lady with whom I spent some time in Tokyo, and her English wasn't very strong. But now that I think of it, this very document testifies to our differences; Jim spends his time musing, but even when I muse I translate those thoughts into activity: I write them down.

I went down to the Conneaut Creek to a point just below the Sherburne Bridge, and watched for a while. The creek is still flowing, but no one is fishing. You can see the lights of Lottsville, Pennsylvania, on the other side; a town that, they tell me, has increased in size tenfold in a score of years. Something about taxes, I understand. Death and taxes, they say, are the only things one can depend on, but I've never paid any taxes.

I walked back—strolled, really—taking my time. I was a little short of money, so I gave some consideration to the problem, but didn't do anything about it. Money is not difficult to come by. I made my way to the Ave, west of the Tunnel, and found an establishment called Cullpepper's. I didn't go in, but I spent a few minutes watching the girls ply their trade. It must be cold, I thought. And they looked so young.

After a while, I picked one out and got acquainted with her for a few minutes. Her name was Rosalie, and she can't have been more than eighteen. She had fair hair, a fair complexion, and was the least bit plump. She was heavily rouged to cover over some minor acne that I think would have made her face more interesting if she'd let it show.

I escorted her home, then returned home myself, cold and not entirely satisfied, but feeling better for having been out, at least. Jim is nowhere in sight, presumably he's wandering around the house, which he does fairly often; it goes with the job, I guess. It's getting late and I'm tired. I'll see Jill tomorrow.

A slight thaw, not uncommon in late December, I'm told, had melted some of the snow from the boulevards and lawns, but it was freezing again as I reached the big white house with the blue lights in the attic. I politely knocked at the door, and, after a minute or so, Jill opened it. Her face went through a quick flurry of contending emotions when she saw me, ending with a small smile. "Hello, Jack," she said.

I walked in past her and threw my coat onto a chair. Susan wasn't in. "Hello yourself. What's this I hear about you seeing Young Don?"

"Where did you hear that?"

"Is it true?"

She frowned. "Jack," she said, "it isn't like we have a relationship."

That stopped me cold. "We haven't?"

"No." She started to pick up strength. "I like you, but that—"

"It seems I've spent an evening in your bed."

She pressed her lips together and tossed her head back. "So?"

"Isn't that a relationship?"

"You mean, sleeping with someone once or twice means you're having a relationship with them?"

I tried to make sense of that. I said, "What do you mean by 'relationship'?"

"I mean, you know, when you're seeing someone regularly, and the two of you always do things together, and—"

"Oh. Excuse me. I didn't understand. No, as you define it, I don't think we're having a relationship."

"Well then?"

"But I forbid you to see Don again."

You'd think I'd just announced that I intended to burn down her house. Her mouth fell open and she stared at me, then she said *"What?"* in a voice that sounded like highland pipes.

I repeated myself.

She said, "Who do you think you are—"

"You will do what you're told," I said.

"I will not—"

"Let's talk about it upstairs."

If anything, that made it worse. "If you think I'm going upstairs with you—"

I shrugged. "Right here will be fine, but won't you be embarrassed if your roommate comes in?"

"If you think I'm going to—"

I laughed, and took her in my arms. She tried to fight her way out, with profound lack of effect. She stopped fighting and said, "Jack, Jack, please stop. This isn't—"

"Keep still," I said, and threw her onto the couch, and myself onto her. She gasped as the air was driven from her lungs. By the time she could speak again she had nothing to say.

Sometime later I looked at her face, tear-streaked and pale. She reached up to caress me clumsily then let her hand fall back down to her side. "Jack?" she said in a whisper.

"Hmmm?"

"I don't—I don't think I can make it up the stairs."

"What's wrong with sleeping on the couch?"

"Please, Jack. I don't want Susan to see me this way."

"You should have thought of that when I first suggested we go upstairs."

She tried to sob but seemed not to have the strength. "Please, Jack."

I sighed. "Very well." I picked her up, carried her upstairs, and put her to bed.

I've had to get up and walk around a little. I've spent some time wandering and seeing what's here. As I was pacing through the house I met Jim in the parlor, his usual haunt, so to speak.

"You've been type-typing away, haven't you?"

"I guess so."

"May I read it?"

"No. Wait, yes. Go ahead. Only don't talk to me about it."

(He's going to be reading this. Will knowing that I have a reader change what I write? I hope not. If I think it does, I'll ask Jim not to read it any more. Hi, Jim, how's the ghost business?)

"I won't," he said. (You said? How can anyone write for an audience? To Hell with it.)

So he went up and read it, and after about an hour came back down. He said, "I don't understand what this Laura Kellem is waiting for. If she's going to stick it to you, why doesn't she just do it?"

I had to think, because I hadn't wondered about it one way or the other. I finally said, "I should imagine that she has quite a bit to work out."

"You said something like that before, but what do you mean?"

"Implicating someone for a murder he didn't commit isn't easy, modern forensics being what it is. If the authorities should discover my name, and succeed in tracing my movements, they might learn that I hadn't arrived in this part of the country until after the crimes had been committed."

He frowned his particular frown, squinching his face as if to touch his eyebrows to his upper lip. "But that means she has to kill you."

"Well, yes, but that isn't difficult, for her. The hard part is bringing in the authorities at just the right time so they think they have their man, and then what they end up with is a body shot full of holes, or burned enough to be unrecognizable. Things don't look good for your abode, Jim."

"So she's out there setting it up right now?"

"Probably."

He frowned very hard, the same frown, as if he were trying to think and it was an effort. In fact, thinking comes pretty naturally to Jim. At last he said, "It seems like something that tricky, you could screw up for her pretty easy."

"In one sense, yes. There are many ways to disrupt it, the simplest being to leave."

"But then—"

"But I can't. She is who she is, and I am who I am, and orders are orders."

He squinted at me. "You don't need to provide examples of the law of identity. I don't understand why you can't—"

"Because I can't. Drop it."

"All right, but couldn't a friend of yours do it?"

"What friend?"

"Well, this Jill person you've been seeing?"

"That'd be no different than me doing it."

"What about if I were to do something?"

"Like what? What can you do? Shit, Jim, you can't even pick up a piece of paper."

He winced at the obscenity and said, "I don't know."

"Neither do I."

"So, what, you're just going to wait for the ax?"

Once more I had to stop and consider the question. I said, "I'm being very careful where I put my feet."

"What d'you mean?"

"I mean that I have to watch where I go, where I'm seen in public, and who I'm seen with. If I were, for example, to kill someone, I'd better make sure there's no one who can trace me to the killing. That kind of thing; trying not to make the job easier for her."

He shook his head. "Can you talk to her about it? She must have cared for you once."

"Cared for me?" I said. "Cared for me?"

"Well, from what you said—"

"You just don't get it, do you? She doesn't care for people the way you mean it. She—"

"Hasn't she ever?"

I started to say "No, she never has," but then I remembered that incident in London. This was before we left for the Continent, so everything was still young and fresh, and I was delighting in my life with her. On that occasion, I went to a cabaret hoping to meet her, and I saw her there, in one of the dark corners, talking earnestly to a young man. I was about to leave, but she caught my eye, and came over to me. We chatted about inconsequential things for a while, then I turned to go. She asked why I was leaving, and I said I thought she was busy. She said she was never too busy for me, and we left together. I never spoke about it, and I didn't even think about it much, but I've never been able to make sense of it, unless, for a while, she really did care about me. I don't know.

Jim was looking at me and waiting for an answer as all of this went through my mind, so I said, "I don't know, maybe she did at one time. But it doesn't matter."

"I guess I just don't understand," he said.

"I guess you just don't," I told him, which ended the conversation.

I'm feeling sort of lazy, so I probably won't go out any more today, unless this machine inspires me the way it did before. Thinking back, that's still a little strange.

There are a few boxes of books in the attic, and I spent some time digging through them. Old boxes of other people's books are always interesting, even if the books themselves aren't, and here there were a few that caught my eye, such as a 1933 edition of the *Encyclopedia Britannica* that I looked at for a while. It seemed to specialize in world history, and I was surprised at how much they got right. I also found ten volumes of "Great Orations," published in 1899. They were in much worse shape than the encyclopedias, but I allowed myself the luxury of a couple of hours with them.

There were plenty of newer books, too, but I feel about books much the way I feel about music; if it's still being printed in fifty years, I'll read it then. If, of course, I'm still around in fifty years, but there's no point in dwelling on that. I'd rather remember Zola's speech to the jury on the Dreyfus case, which I found in Volume 10. I don't know who recorded that speech for history, but he ought to be thanked.

Certainly, there's a good deal of nonsense in it. "Who suffers for truth and justice becomes august and sacred." Indeed? I remember laughing aloud the first time I read that, and wishing I'd been there when he said it just so I could have looked at his face and seen if he believed it. But there is some truth in his speech that goes far beyond the case of the moment, and his love for his military, and his worship of that stupid country full of stupid Frenchmen. "For when folly and lies are thus sown broadcast, you necessarily reap insanity," he said, and what man who has lived for more than forty years has not seen that truth?

"We have had to fight step by step against an extraordinarily obstinate desire for darkness." Yes, indeed, Emile, we have; or, rather, you have, you and your ilk. That is certainly not my fight, nor will it ever be, but I can applaud yours, and even, to my surprise, discover a couple of tears for the way it has been fought. And, do you know, sometimes I even think that some ground has been gained. But then I read, in Volume 6, Robert Emmet's speech from the scaffold, and I remember that Great Britain has banned songs that might even hint that all is not well in Northern Ireland, and I see that darkness is reclaiming its own.

But, as I said, this has never been my fight, and never will be. Darkness, I think, has its own charm, as long as one can see well enough to avoid tripping over the furniture. As for me, my only desire is the quite natural one to live; to continue my chain of existence. And even that doesn't matter much to me. That is a strange thing to say, but it has been going through my head since Jim brought it up, and it seems to me that I continue to exist, and I enjoy it, but should the end come, as it might soon, I will meet it with a shrug. This is no great virtue, nor any great flaw, it is simply my nature, and what man can contend with his nature?

But there, too—this is a strength. Zola and Emmet notwithstanding, strength does not come from passion for justice, it comes from not caring—about life, about justice, or what have you. If you are able to face an enemy, and not care what he does to you, then he cannot really hurt you. If you are able to say to a lover, "Do this or I'll leave you," and your lover wants you to stay, then you have power; it's that simple. If you are able to say to the judge, "Kill me if you want, I don't care," and the judge doesn't want to kill you, then you have the power. Now, it may be that the lover wants to leave you, and the judge probably does want to kill you, but if you can say, "I don't care," that is a strength they cannot take away.

Of course, you must mean it.

I seem to have reached a state where I can say these things and mean them, and it is this power that I enjoy. That is why I don't fear what Kellem may do. Certainly, I cannot escape her, in this she has the power. But because that doesn't matter to me, because I don't care if I live or die, she cannot really hurt me.

No one can hurt me.

But I can still shed a few tears for Emile Zola.

Another day gone by. The weather has turned very cold, and the lack of heating in the house (the thermostat is set just barely high enough to keep the pipes from freezing) is becoming annoying. I have the choice of sitting in front of the fireplace or here at the typewriter. My fingers are actually cold enough to interfere with my typing, at least a little. It just occurred to me that I could bring this machine down to the parlor, but I don't think I want to. And there's a limit to how often we ought to have a fire; the house is known to be deserted, and I'd hate to have someone come by to investigate why smoke is coming from the chimney.

I'm feeling well just now—very well. I stopped by to visit Jill, but she was flat on her back with, she said, some sort of virus. She warned me not to come too close or I'd be likely to catch it. I took the chance of giving her a quick peck on the forehead, which felt warm but not feverish, then went downstairs.

Susan was wearing a plain black ankle-length skirt that tied at the waist and a white T-shirt that didn't advertise anything. She was stretched out on the couch, her feet up on some cushions, reading a magazine called Z. She pivoted her neck backward so she was looking at me upside down and said, "I didn't hear you come in."

"I was checking on Jill. She's sick."

"Yes, I know." She sat up and twisted around in one motion.

"It's a little cold outside," I said, "but we can call a cab, if you wish."

"You want to go out?"

"We might."

"We could order a pizza."

"None for me; I'd just been thinking coffee."

"If that's all, shall I put some on? I have Kona."

"Good idea, and you can order a pizza for yourself. I'll watch you eat it and make helpful suggestions."

I studied her walk as she went back into the kitchen. She turned her head and gave me a big smile. Presently there was the sound of a coffee grinder. I looked through her record collection. She seemed to be a holdout, judging from the lack of CDs. But records are more fun to look through anyway. There seemed to be no logic to the arrangement, with Mozart stuck between The Clash and Kate Bush and so on, but the real surprise was the number of musicals; a quick glance showed me *Oklahoma!*, *The Music Man, West Side Story,* and *South Pacific.* Interesting.

Coffee smells began to permeate the room. I put on a collection of Scott Joplin rags. There is something indefinable about Joplin that reminds me of the tunes I used to hear the fiddlers play back in the proverbial Old Country. I'm not sure what it is, but when the sounds of the upright piano filled the room, I felt it.

"Feel free to put something on the stereo," she called.

"Thanks, I will."

She waltzed back, twirled twice, bent backward with one arm curled over her head, straightened, bent forward, picked up the telephone, pushed buttons from memory, and ordered a small pizza with pepperoni, onions, and mushrooms. She spoke on the telephone as if ordering this pizza was one of the most exciting things she had ever done.

As she was hanging up, the door opened, and a very young looking couple, both wearing old ankle-length coats, scarves, and stocking caps, came in, accompanied by a trace of cold air in spite of the entryway door. They looked at me, I looked back. Susan introduced them as the mysterious tenants of the attic as they took off their winter garb and set things on pegs in the entryway. Neither of them commented on my bobby's coat. She was a little taller than he was, had mousy brown hair and a rounded face with tiny blue eyes. He looked like a New York Jew, with long, curly dark hair, faintly Semitic features and brown eyes. Her name was Melissa and his was Tom. They looked and acted burned out. I smelled stale marijuana smoke on their clothes (her T-shirt said Hard Rock Cafe, Chicago, his said Pink Floyd), but that proved nothing; it's possible to burn out on marijuana, but it takes dedication. Susan told them my name and it looked as if it had passed through her head, into his, and then fallen to the floor; I'd have been willing to bet money that if I had asked them what it was right then neither would have known.

Tom sniffled, Julie coughed, and they headed up the stairs after nodding to me politely.

"Now I understand," I said.

Her eyebrows asked the obvious.

"The blue lights in the attic," I explained. "All has become clear. Do they manage their share of the rent on time?"

"His mother owns the house," she said. "We pay him."

"I see. Not a bad arrangement, I guess."

"They're okay. There was a while when they were using ecstasy, and—"

"Ecstasy?"

"MDMA. A designer hallucinogen. They were a little hard to live with then because they wanted Jill and me to understand how wonderful we really were." She laughed. "Jill took to hiding in her room and I started playing speed metal. Anyway, now they're back to acid, and at least we can stand that." She turned her head sideways, I suppose to gauge my reaction, as she said, "I've tripped with them a couple of times."

She seemed to be waiting for me to say something, so I said, "I've never used, myself."

"Want to sometime?"

"Not really." After all, it either wouldn't affect me, or it would, right? "Does it matter?"

"No," she said. "I think it does not."

"I agree. And in any case there's something more important to us."

"Oh? What's that?"

"Your pizza is here."

She laughed. "That *is* more important, but I don't hear anything."

"You will."

The door chime came right on cue; two deep-throated gongs, the second a fifth below the first. She looked quizzically at me and said, "You have good hearing."

"I only listen to quiet music."

She stood up and went over to the mantelpiece, took the top off a pewter bowl, and pulled some paper money out of it. "Then turn the record over and we'll hear some more. Coffee should be done, too; help yourself."

I turned over the record and got two cups of coffee, mine only half full, so I missed hearing her interactions with the delivery boy; that would have been interesting. The coffee steamed on the knee-high table in front of the couch. There were coasters on it, so I used them. She set the box down, opened it, and said, "Are you sure you don't want any?"

"Quite sure. I'll just make you nervous by watching you eat." In fact, I thought the smell rising from the baked dough more noxious than appetizing, but I kept my opinion to myself. I brought the coffee to my lips, enjoying the warmth, as Susan took a triangular piece of pizza and bit into it. Her bites were neither gluttonous nor dainty; she seemed to be enjoying herself.

"So," she said as she finished the first piece and carefully wiped her mouth on a paper napkin furnished by the pizza company, "you like Joplin?"

"That contumelious ass? Hardly."

"What do you mean?"

I smiled. "Excuse me, I was being funny. Yes, I

enjoy his music a great deal. You, it seems, have quite a variety of taste."

"And you don't?"

"In theory, yes. I like the very best music, whatever form it might take."

"But?"

"But I haven't the patience to wade through the ninety-nine percent that is worthless to find the occasional gem, so I usually let time decide for me."

She frowned. "What do you mean?"

"If a piece of music has survived forty or fifty years, then it probably has something to it that is worth listening to."

She shook her head. "You have to wait a long time, then, to hear anything new."

"I'm patient," I said. "And the music I enjoy does not quickly become wearisome."

"I love the way you talk," she said, smiling full into my face.

"More coffee?"

"Please."

I got her a new cup, warmed my own. She drank some, had another piece of pizza, then closed the box and said, "I think that is enough for me."

"Then shall we go upstairs?"

"By all means." She stood and held out her hand for mine. I took it, and, believe this if you will, I felt anticipation like a quickening of the pulse and a shortness of the breath. We went past the room where Jill was sleeping soundly, and Susan opened the door to her room. She stepped in, turned the overhead light on, and I followed. I took a moment to observe, both for what I could learn of her, and to prolong the moment; to hold off the delicious and now inevitable joining; if I ever indulge myself shamelessly, I think it is in such things as this.

It was a good-sized room, with walls painted some

color for which only women know the name, one of those shades that is almost white with a bit of yellow. On the wall to my right was a black-framed photograph of her in the midst of some dance, ecstatic expression, mid-leap, etc. The opposite wall held a print of Renoir's *Moulin de la Galette*. There were potted plants both hanging and on the floor throughout the room, many of them trailing tendrils haphazardly, so one had the impression that the entire room was framed in green stems and leaves. The end of one even dangled onto a corner of the bed, which was a mattress set on the floor, in elegant disarray of blue pillows, blue sheets, and yellow comforter. A plain wood dresser was next to it, an old-fashioned windup alarm clock on the dresser.

"Do you like it?" she said, spinning slowly, arm extended to show the room.

"Yes, only I'd expected a big iron bed enclosed in white lace."

"Oh yes. Someday."

She pulled off her T-shirt with the unselfconsciousness one finds in actors and, I suppose, dancers. There was no trace of coquetry in the action, although she watched me and smiled. She wore nothing underneath. She untied her skirt, let it fall, and stepped out of it. She wore nothing underneath that, either.

I searched for an interjection and didn't find one, so I just shook my head. She came up to me and began unbuttoning my shirt. I took her hands in mine and held them, then brought my mouth to her warm, warm lips. She seemed startled by the contact at first, then relaxed. Our tongues touched for an instant, then I pulled back and our eyes met. Hers were very wide and deep, inviting me to become lost in them as she became lost in mine. I put my arms around her, my hand finding the hollow of her back as I kissed her temple, her ear, and her neck. We sank down onto the bed, still holding each other.

I ran my hands along her body. Yes, indeed, she was a dancer, or an acrobat, or a swimmer. She was strong, inside and out. I touched her and she shivered; she touched me and I trembled. I felt her enter the maelstrom of sensation at the same time I did, and we explored it together. She made low, moaning sounds of pleasure, while mine were harsh and animallike, but the urgency was mutual.

Many, many hours later I rose. She was sleeping soundly, with a slight smile on her face. I slipped out of the house and returned to my own. Jim said something when I came in, but I don't remember what it was. I only shook my head in answer and came up here to stare at a blank page and let the cold seep back into my body. I am still in a daze from the experience, one of the most powerful of my life. It is as if I have changed in some way, but I can't tell what it is, or if it will fade with time.

Change frightens me, and it is a long time since I have been frightened. I don't know what this means, but I do not like it.

FOUR

flinch *intr.v.* 1. To betray fear, pain, or surprise with an involuntary gesture such as a start; to wince. 2. To draw away; retreat.

AMERICAN HERITAGE DICTIONARY

What is love? I think

I must not see Susan any more. If I

Happy New Year, Jim. How should we

What is Kellem doing? Why haven't I heard from her? Or, more accurately, why hasn't she consummated her scheme? It has been more than a month, and this waiting is

I haven't touched this machine for several days, and, now that I am here, I find myself both reluctant and unable to set down what I have been doing. I have not been back to see Susan or Jill; in fact I have been doing very little except walking around and around the house, occasionally venturing out into the yard, sometimes the street.

I find myself growing apprehensive at the prospect

of what Kellem has planned. There is no doubt that she is pulling together all the threads for my demise, and the thought of her complacently going about her business, knowing she may take as much time as she needs, has been preying on my mind. And yet, she is certainly right, there is nothing I can do.

It is mid-January, and winter's grip is still firm. I must be careful where I walk, lest I leave footprints that could cause suspicion. My thoughts have returned to Susan several times, but I don't think it means anything; little infatuations are not uncommon, particularly in old men, and no doubt it will pass. I remember that, years ago, Kellem mentioned something about this, although I can't think what it was. I recall that we were walking as she spoke, and it must have been shortly after we left London, because that was when we spent the most time together, and she was telling me things I ought to watch out for, and she mentioned infatuations as one.

I said, "Why should I worry about that when I have you to be infatuated with?" She laughed, treating it as a joke, so I pushed it a little and said, "Is that what I am? A little infatuation?" and that made her laugh even more. It's funny how I see all of these clear signs now, but never saw them when they were happening. There's probably a moral in there somewhere, but I don't think I'll bother trying to find it.

I have been avoiding Jill because, I suppose, of some fear of involvement with Susan, but the notion is absurd. Tomorrow I will visit Jill.

I must say that I am growing to like Jim; it seems we are saying more with fewer words. Our conversations over the past few days have been short, and seldom about anything, but they have been a source of distraction and no small solace as I go through this period of anguish about Kellem's plans. Certainly, I don't expect it to last—there is little that is more senseless than bothering one's self over what cannot be helped, and it is quite unusual for me to worry about anything.

It is one of those days when the path of the moon matches the sun, and it comes with the new moon. There used to be those who believed that this was a time of change, or growth, and, who knows, maybe there is some truth in it.

Today I thought I would go back to the Ave and perhaps pick up a girl, but apparently the best, as it were, had been taken; those who were left were the old ones, or those who played too hard at appearing glamorous, or coy, and after a time one gets tired of these things.

I am tempted to rail at the stupidity of women, did I not know that these theatrics are perpetrated because of the stupidity of men. And, in all honesty, I was no better myself when I was younger. It comes to me that Prudence, the girl I nearly married, was of just this type. Odd. I have not thought of Prudence in some time, and now that I do, I cannot see what attraction she ever held for me. Her laugh, which I remember as so endearing, was in fact a stupid titter, and there was no trace of life in her smile, nor did she ever say anything that could have held the interest of anyone.

I've heard women, and, lately, some men, talk of women acting stupid to please men, but in fact, I think, that is not what they are doing; it is not lack of wit or intellect that shallow men crave, it is lack of personality; they desire a woman who will exist only as a shadow to themselves, because this gives them the illusion that they have some importance, that they are more than cattle. Personality is what distinguishes us from each other, what makes each man and woman unique, and to submerge one's personality is to make one's self interchangeable, like a mass-produced commodity; yet the demands of instinct, the will to survive through reproduction, are strong, and if this is what it takes to fulfill that instinct, not many can fight it. But really, why should I care? Most men, in fact, are little more than cattle, as are most women. When one finds an exception, such as

I am rambling pointlessly, a sure sign that the fingers have become disconnected from the frontal lobes. It feels very late, and, though we are past the solstice, I am nevertheless feeling an acute need for sleep. Tomorrow I will visit Jill, and no doubt I will feel better for it, and if I wish then to set down more words, perhaps there will be some thought behind them.

My hands have twitched over the keys a few times. I want to write, but it feels as if I've been in a place of dreams, and everything is still in that state midway between the time of sleeping and the time of waking; when the distinction between the real and the unreal either doesn't exist or cannot be found. Show me a painting by Salvador Dalí, and I might like it now; or at least I might understand it. Time has stretched, so that a few hours are an age; and it has collapsed, so that the events of hours seem to have ended before they began. Turmoil, even when generated from within, can do that to a person.

But, in fact, I think that little has really happened; I have gone from acute worry (has Kellem's trap been sprung? would the police show up while I slept?) to rage, to—well, through the whole range of emotions, but all of these momentous events were internal; in fact, I have done little.

No gentlemen in blue came to disturb me, so when I got up I walked down to the booth at the corner and reached my dear Gillian by telephone and asked her to meet me. She said she would rather not.

"Why is that?" I said into the cold, black plastic. "Are you unwell?"

"No, I'm feeling fine, thanks." Her voice was strange over the phone, forced and artificial.

"Then what is it?"

"I have to study."

"You can study later. Right now I have something for you to do."

"No, I really can't. I'm sorry." She hung up before I could say anything more, so I went over there. I entered just as she was walking out the door, apparently in a hurry. When she saw me, she stopped and looked guilty, as if she'd been caught at something.

"Where are you going?" I said.

"Nowhere," she said.

"Good. Then there's something you can help me with."

"Jack—"

"Let's go."

I had her help me find the offices of the *Lakota Plainsman,* which we did just before they closed. I put an ad in the personals that read, "Laura K, Jack wants to see you." I was running short of cash, so I had Jill pay for it. She complained of the headache, so I took her home after that. The stars twinkled benignly as we walked, with no moon to kick them back into supporting roles.

She said, "Did you sleep with Susan?"

"Yes."

"Why?"

"I wanted to."

"I don't think—"

"Then don't speak."

"Jack—"

"Shut up."

She huddled into herself and we completed the walk in as much silence as the night would allow, with its chatter of night things and occasional automobiles. I escorted her through the door and didn't touch her except to help her take off her coat; I am nothing if not a gentleman. Susan was not in; no doubt she was dancing or perhaps out with some friends. I went off alone. Sometimes I let my Wellingtons slap against the sidewalk, sometimes I made my footfalls silent. It was cold, colder than New York at any rate; but it was a distant cold; it didn't really penetrate, rather it tingled against my cheeks and inside my nose. I came to a place called Terrence F. Kleffman Park. It was one neat city block, surrounded by evenly spaced oaks, with a wading pool in the middle, and a pair of baseball diamonds at the far end, identified by those peculiar tall wire fences to catch the balls the players miss. Here, said the park, you may engage in recreation during the prescribed hours. Here are the trees you may be shaded by, and these are the sports in which you may participate.

There had been a light snowfall during the day, and a little bit remained in the grass of the park, making it look like a field of toothpicks sticking up out of a sandbox filled with salt.

A police cruiser went by on the far side. They didn't notice me, or they would certainly have sent a spotlight my way, and maybe stopped to ask questions. What could someone be doing alone in a park at night in the middle of winter? Must be something illegal. Ah, you poor fools, walking so tall and haughty with your guns and your sticks and your wide belts full of gear like the second coming of Batman, sitting in your little cars full of mechanized fear as you reach for your little radios at the first sign of anything more worrisome than a jaywalker. Shall I introduce you to Jim? How would you feel about that, you blue-jacketed clowns? But he's nothing, of course. What about Traci, who lives less than a hundred miles from here, and, when the mood is on her, could walk through a storm of your metal-coated lead-filled man-killers, and rip your heart out and eat it in front of you before you died? Yes, drive on, drive on, looking for drunks on the road or children out past curfew. You are nothing to me.

Oh, I have no doubt Kellem means to use you to bring me to earth, but, even then, you will be no more than tools. That's all you will ever be, faceless, nameless tools, who sell yourselves more often and more cheaply than any whore in this town.

I began to run, which I often do when frustration turns to wrath. The icy wind stroked my hair like Laura's caress had, so long, so long ago. The pavement hurt my feet, but that didn't slow me. My senses were filled with the mindless, meaningless life I passed; my heart was full of the need for destination, which I found, and that filled me; now I wished for a moon to light my way, for my sight had dimmed, but all of my other senses were heightened. I wanted to laugh, but in my range it was another sound that emerged, but no one heard it anyway, or ever would, for silence inhabits the minds of the deaf, and mine is the power over those who will not hear.

> Shadows slowly lengthen as evening turns to
>   cold;
> The fruits of my labor lie dormant in the
>   hold.
> An empty hand awaits a glove another day
>   survived,
> Nightmares fall like poetry, carefully
>   contrived.
> The leaves blow 'round in circles where
>   before the sun was hot,
> Add a pinch of desperation to what's boiling
>   in the pot.
> The circle widens now, with every blinded
>   turn and twist,
> To tell of wind and thunder, ice and rain and
>   mist.

Close your coat against the wind, tight
    around your neck;
It's bitter here without the sun, but what did
    you expect?
Words flow by like melody; watch as they
    unfold,
And hear the shadows lengthen as evening
    turns to cold.

For the first time in more years than I care to remember,
I've written a poem. I must have spent four or five hours
revising it, then typed it out all nice and neat, and I still
don't really like it; it seems like one of those regular,
choppy efforts made by first-year students of English
literature; but it is interesting that I felt like attempting
poetry at all. I think it is this house that is bringing out
that side of me. I stopped by to see Jill again today, but
she wasn't in, and neither was Susan. I have nothing to
say, but sitting here is better than anything else I can
think of to do. Maybe I'll go back to Jill's place again
and wait around until she comes home. Or I

Jim has just come in and suggested we build a fire.
We haven't had one in several days, and perhaps that is
the better idea. I shall sit in front of the fire and ask Jim
to tell me of the house; who has lived here and why they
left. If he is not in a mood to talk, I shall stare into the
flames the way he does, and maybe I'll begin to learn
what he is seeing in the dancing lights.

It has reached the point where I become annoyed when,
like yesterday, I can't get to the typing machine. Odd
how much this annoys me. Didn't Horatio say something
on the subject? Or was it Hamlet? My education seems to
be gradually slipping away. This saddens me. I was once
a very good student, I think. I had a good attitude,
which, I believe, means that one looks on learning as a

game; or rather, a series of games, such as: What can I invent as a device to remember the year the War of the Roses ended? Or, how can I use my studies of German philosophy to help with a paper on natural science?

Now that I think of it, I cannot remember when the War of the Roses ended, and the little I remember of German philosophy is that a few of us once wrote a poem about an imaginary duel between Feuerbach and Hegel, which the latter eventually won by putting the former to sleep and then drowning him in a twenty-page sentence. It sounds more clever than it probably was, but we were pleased with it at the time, although we never dared to show it to our professors.

Nevertheless, I think I was a good student. I have, at any rate, retained a strong desire to learn, and a tendency to question things around me. I've been told that age brings acceptance and complacency, and I've even seen examples of this, but it seems not to be true in my case.

Age does, however, bring about an annoying softening of the hard edges of memory; there are now many things of which I no longer remember the details, only how those details affected me. I remember a Latin professor named Smythe, and I have the feeling that he was a devoutly religious man, yet kind and well disposed toward me, but I can no longer remember what he looked like, nor any of the things he actually did. This annoys me.

As I said, I was not able to use the typewriting machine yesterday, because the house was invaded just as I was about to come up to my sanctum. It was not a serious, nor even frightening invasion; there were three boys, aged about ten or eleven, who, from what little I picked up of their conversation, had been dared or had dared each other to spend a night in the haunted house.

I kept urging Jim to make himself visible to them, or

let me rattle some woodwork or something, but he wouldn't. We sat in the basement with the dust and the spiders and occasionally went up to see if they were still there.

"You like children, don't you?" I said.

"Used to be one," said Jim.

"Would you have spent a night in a haunted house?"

"No, sir, not for anything."

"I think I might have, if we'd had one around."

"I would have thought that haunted houses were everywhere."

"Not as such. We knew ghosts appeared, here and there, but mostly in places we couldn't get to. And there were always a few spirits of one sort or another in everyone's house, or at least we thought there were, but I don't remember anyone ever leaving a house because there was a spirit there. Then, in England—"

"When did you go to England?"

"I was sent to University there. In England there were stories of ghosts in nearly every building on the campus, I think, but I can't recall any in houses."

"These kids got some grit, though," he said.

"Maybe. We could find out for sure if you'd—"

"No."

"Have it your way. I'm going to take a walk."

"Can you get out of the house without them seeing you?"

"Is that a joke?"

"Yes."

"Enjoy the basement."

I wandered for a while, something I was getting good at, but did nothing of interest beyond making some very general plans for the next day.

Laura Kellem was waiting near the front door, apparently having determined that I wasn't home. Her head was uncovered, and, while she had no more hair missing, there were still those odd bald patches. They made her look slightly grotesque, which in an odd way enhanced her attractiveness.

When she saw me, the first thing she said was, "What was it you wanted to see me about that drove you to place an ad in the personals, of all things?"

"It worked. How else could I see you? You've carefully arranged things so all communication is one-way."

"Well, I'm here. Shall we go inside?"

"Sorry, company."

"Excuse me?"

"Some children have shown up to see if they could spend the night in the haunted house."

Kellem laughed.

"Not so loudly, if you please," I said.

She nodded, still grinning. "Is your ghost friend doing anything to their poor, dear heads?"

"No; he's showing great restraint."

"What are they doing now?"

"I've been out. When I left they were lighting a fire in the fireplace and talking about telling ghost stories. I wonder if they'll notice that the fireplace has been used lately."

"I doubt it."

She looked around at the yard, so overgrown with weeds that one could see them above the snow, surrounded by a faded, rotting fence that had once been painted red, featuring, on one side of the now invisible walk, a single apple tree of the variety someone had once called Mushy Rome Beauty, and, on the other, a catalpa with enough twists to give the place a creepy feeling even if it didn't have Jim to lend it authenticity. "A nice place, actually," said Kellem.

"Yes. A good location, too; not far from St. Bart's, not far from the Tunnel, a couple of parks nearby. It was built by a professor of one of the colleges, I forget which, right around the turn of the century."

"Why was it abandoned?"

"Last family to buy it thought it was haunted. They wouldn't live there, and refused to sell it to anyone else without the guarantee that it would be torn down. The Historical Society wouldn't let that happen, even if they'd found someone stupid enough to do it."

"So here it sits," she said.

"Yes. From time to time the city comes in and cleans up the yard and sends the owners a bill. As long as they pay the taxes, no one cares."

She looked at me fully. "What do you want?"

"I would like," I said, "to negotiate."

"Pardon me?"

I repeated myself.

She shook her head. "I don't understand. For what?"

"Eh? For my life."

It seemed to get through at last, and she looked like she didn't know if she ought to laugh or just look perplexed. "What would you have that I might want? Or that I couldn't get anyway?"

"I don't know," I said. "Can we discuss it?"

"You're wasting my time."

"I just want—"

"Quiet," she said, and I was quiet. Her eyes pinned me in place, then forced me down, first to my knees, then onto my face in the snow. It was very cold, and it came to me with a sense of rage that I would not be able to stand in front of the fire because of those damned children. I should have liked to have slaughtered them, but Jim would never have forgiven me.

"You have nothing to say to me," said Kellem. "I have decided your fate, and that is an end of it. You will wait, no more. That is all."

When I looked up she had gone.

I was, as I said, unable to type yesterday because of the children, so I may have left out some details. In any case, they were gone when I awoke, and I trust they will not return.

FIVE

en·er·gy *n.* 1.a. Vigor or power in action. b. Vitality and intensity of expression. 2. The capacity for action or accomplishment: *lacked energy to finish the job.*

AMERICAN HERITAGE DICTIONARY

I've been sitting here remembering things.

The last time I saw Laura Kellem was in County Mayo, Ireland, perhaps a score of years ago. I had been living in London, which seems to be the place in all the world I keep coming back to. I don't remember exactly where I'd found digs, but it was probably either Soho or the East End, because that's where I've been most often.

I remember that for several months I'd been feeling listless, careless, and generally uninterested in life. I didn't know, then, that I was, to some degree, subject to whatever moods Kellem might be having, at least if they were intense. If I'd known that, I'd have probably been expecting something like what happened. As it was, I didn't even realize what was happening to me until much later, when I reconstructed the events.

I slowly began to get the feeling I would like to leave England—an idea that grew stronger and stronger over the course of about a week. Then the feeling became more specific, in that I was taken by a wish to see Ireland. I realized what was going on, and allowed it to happen because there was nothing I could do, and I never minded seeing Laura anyway.

So I went to her, where she was living in a small house, almost like a cottage, outside of the town of Ballina, in the province of Connaught in the west of the Republic of Ireland. It was beautiful country, full of broken, craggy rocks and seacoast, but I saw little of it. I was guided to her doorstep, which fact was unusual in itself, and then she let me in. While she was not living in complete squalor, I don't think the floor had been swept for months, nor had anything been dusted. She seemed very, very old; I would have taken her for an eighty- or ninety-year old woman, and it seemed that the effort of walking to the door and back to her chair was almost too much for her; the fire had all but gone out of her eyes.

I said, "What's happened to you, Kellem?" But I could see what had happened: lethargy, self-neglect, weakness.

When she spoke, I could barely hear her. She said, "Jack, help me."

So I did. I cleaned up the place, which took a couple of days, and then I went to the local pub and got acquainted with a few residents. Eventually I found a fine, strong-looking young man with a booming laugh and pearly-white teeth who was willing to follow me home and keep drinking after the pub closed. I introduced him to my "grandmother," and fed him Scotch whisky, his secret passion, until he burbled, hiccuped, and passed out in his chair.

Of course, Laura became drunk too, which I'd never seen before, and I think that did as much good as anything else. She began breaking up the place, after which she slept for two days, by which time the constabulary were nosing around us and we had to leave the vicinity.

Kellem went on to Dublin, while I, at her sugges-
tion, returned once more to America, and so we went our
separate ways, but when we parted she seemed a changed
woman—her fire was back, and she had learned how to
laugh once more, as if she had drawn it out of the young
man.

Her train left first, and I stood with her at the station
and waited for it. She squeezed my hand, and for just a
moment things were again as they had been so many
years before. One part of me realized that it was a facade,
because by then I knew her, but I think, experienced as
I was, I wanted to believe there still remained some trace
of affection for me.

I guess I continued to think so until last night.

I went for nice little walk around the area, and met our
neighbor across the road, although he doesn't know we
are neighbors, and I didn't see fit to enlighten him. He
was walking his dog, a little brown and white terrier. I
was returning to the house and he was approaching me,
and the dog suddenly went into a frenzy, barking at
me, bristling, and growling, until I nearly lost patience
with it.

The owner, a nice old gentleman in his early sixties,
seemed quite embarrassed by the dog's behavior and
apologized profusely, all the while trying to calm the
annoying beast. I bent down and held out my hand for
the dog to sniff, at which time the animal suddenly
backed away and started whimpering, which made the
old man even more apologetic.

"Don't worry about it," I said. "Animals often
don't like me."

"He doesn't usually behave this way—"

"As I said, not to worry."

"Well, thanks. I'm Bill Kowalsky."

"Jack Agyar."

"How d'you do, Jack. Live nearby?"

"Back that way," I said, gesturing vaguely. "I was just taking a walk."

"You must be new around here."

"How did you know?"

"I always take Pepper out after supper, and I haven't seen you before."

"Well, it's a pleasure." Our gloves shook hands.

"You own a house, or rent?"

"Neither one, actually; I'm just visiting."

"Oh? For how long?"

"Hard to say. I'm doing some work at Twain."

"Really? So am I. What field?"

"Oh, just reading some dusty old manuscripts. You?"

"Biology."

"You're a professor?"

"That's right." He laughed. "And I've even published."

"Good for you," I said. "I'm hoping to."

"Oh? What do you want to publish?"

"Summaries of dusty old manuscripts."

He laughed and nodded and asked a few more questions to which I told a few more lies. He ended by suggesting I drop in for coffee, and I told him I'd take him up on that sometime. That's when he pointed out his house, which turned out to be just across the street from ours. I said, "You must be tired of staring at that fence all the time."

"Naw, I kind of like it. The place is supposed to be haunted, you know."

"Really? Do you believe in that kind of thing?"

"No, I'm afraid not. But it really is a wonderful place. You should look at it."

I told him I would, said goodbye, and continued my walk. Bill, I think, didn't give me another thought, but I could feel Pepper watching me all the way down the street.

Tonight it is unusually still outside, as if nature were holding her breath waiting for something to happen. This is not the first time in my long and checkered life that I've had this feeling, and I can never remember it meaning anything; yet I am always affected by the sensation. The early hours of the morning have a kind of loneliness to them that at once attract and repel me.

I am not a loner by disposition. Part of the reason Kellem got into so much trouble in Ireland was that she can be perfectly happy by herself for long periods of time. Of course, her great age and naturally cynical disposition had more to do with it, but still, if she were as I am, surrounded by people as often as possible, laughing and crying with them, drinking in the successes and failures of their lives, I don't think it would have happened.

I suppose that is one reason I am so glad that Jim is here. It's funny, because while this is not the first house I've lived in that was haunted, it is the first where the ghost has been at all communicative. When I first moved to Staten Island, six or seven years ago, I found, as was my custom, a deserted house and at once felt the presence of a very strong spirit. Yet, in all the time I lived there, which is up until last November, when I answered Laura's summons, I never had any contact with whomever or whatever it was; I know no more about it today than I did the day I arrived.

With Jim it was different. I felt his presence right away (indeed, I think I am drawn to places with such phenomena). I made a brief inspection of the lower floors of the house looking for a place to store my luggage, and had settled on a nice corner of the basement, when a voice behind me said, as cool as you please, "There is an old vault behind that bookcase." I think I must have jumped a foot into the air, and if I didn't scream it was purely accidental. I must get Jim to tell me how that looked from his side.

When I turned around, there he was, staring past my shoulder and looking apologetic. "I'm sorry, I really hadn't intended to frighten you," he said, or something like that.

I took a moment to recover myself, then said, "Do you know, it has been so long since I've been frightened by anything that I almost don't mind."

He introduced himself, and so did I, and I asked him how he came to be haunting the place and he just looked uncomfortable, and he asked me what I was doing in Lakota and I shrugged off the question.

He told me how to get into the vault, which turned out to be an old counting room. It was extraordinarily well hidden; even the false wall was much thicker than I'd have expected. It was only just large enough for me and the crate, but it was snug and, after only a few minutes of work, quite clean.

Then I started asking about his life, and it turned out he was even older than I was, and for some reason that endeared him to me; perhaps it made me think of Kellem, who is the only other person I know who can say that.

He seemed desperately anxious to hear about the places I'd been, I suppose because he'd never done much traveling. I was equally anxious to learn what life was like for him in this part of the world, but he didn't seem inclined to discuss it.

The other thing I remember is that, at one point, he was talking about the superstitions among black people of his time (he calls them "Negroes"), and I asked if he shared any of those beliefs, and he seemed genuinely insulted.

He's a fascinating man. On the one hand, he never

really does anything, I guess because of his nature; but on the other, ever since this business with Kellem has come up he's been nagging at me to "do something about it."

And, do you know, I'm beginning, more and more, to think he's right. Perhaps there really isn't anything I can do to stop Kellem—I must obey any order she gives—but I ought at least to try. If I were to be destroyed tomorrow, well, there are things I would miss. I do not really believe in Heaven or in Hell, for if these things were true, why do we so busily create them on Earth? And I do not believe in reincarnation, because if it were true, why would we try so hard to continue our existences, in one way or another, through as much time as possible?

What matters to me are those experiences I can take into my memory to look back on, with pleasure or remorse as the case may be. Maybe that is why this little typewritten journal has become so important and why I've been writing as if I were telling myself a story; it is a way to preserve parts of my memory, which seems to be very gradually fading, or rather, diffusing, as a photograph will when it has been enlarged too many times.

Yes, I am convinced. I must do something. And I think I know what. Tomorrow, then, I will cast aside the remains of this laissez-faire existence, and see what I can do to make at least some gesture toward self-preservation.

If nothing else, it will make the days pass quickly.

I think it was the experience with Kellem that drove me to action, although I'd been thinking about this in general ever since placing the advertisement in the personals for her. I must say I had hoped for a better result from the advertisement.

In any case, upon rising today, I remembered my resolve at once. I sat in the living room stewing for a few minutes, then left the house, made my way to the offices of the *Plainsman* (I don't even remember who or what I met on the way), and entered. There were a few fluorescent lights on in the building, and only one watchman, standing near a door. I didn't use that door so he didn't see me.

It took a while to find what I wanted; there were several floors to search; but eventually I found someone sitting alone in front of a computer screen. He was in his late forties or early fifties, about half of his hair was gone and the rest very short and dark, he had a bit of a potbelly and several hours' growth of whiskers on his heavy face. Maybe he was starting a beard; if I'd had a chin like that, I'd have grown one.

His desk was overflowing with Diet Coke cans, bent paperclips, an ashtray leaking peanut shells, four audio cassettes, a framed photograph of a couple of ugly grammar-school-aged children (no wife shown), a few issues of various news magazines, reference books, and memo pads. He was reading one of the news magazines, and I must have been standing next to him for most of a minute before he noticed me. He wasn't startled, he just looked confused, then he said in a voice that was much higher-pitched than I'd expected, "Who are you?"

"Jack," I said. "Jack Agyar."

"Yeah? What do you want?"

"I need you to dig something up for me on the computer."

"Huh?"

I repeated myself. He still didn't seem to understand. I pointed to the terminal and said, "Start that thing up, I need you to ask it some questions for me."

He looked at me like a Labrador retriever that's been given a command outside its vocabulary. He said, "Who did you say you are?"

I gave him my name again. I can be very patient.

"You work for the paper?"

"No."

He finally seemed to have figured out what was going on. "Then why the hell should I—"

I took him by the throat and lifted him up, so his feet were kicking wildly in the air. He made gurgling sounds, but couldn't get much volume. "Because," I said, "I would appreciate your help."

I dropped him back into his chair and smiled at him. He had a coughing jag, and when it was over I noticed that he was covered with sweat and stank badly. He just stared at me until I pointed to the screen. "Now," I said. "I'm in a hurry."

He nodded, wide-eyed, and turned to the screen. His hands were shaking. He typed a space, and the screen, which had been blank, became filled with nonsense, some of it almost in English. There was a blinking line in front of a copyright symbol at the bottom of the screen. He typed "call out library," stopping to correct several errors in his typing. It said, "Login." He typed something I couldn't see because it didn't appear on the screen, then the copyright symbol came back on.

"What do you want to find?" he squeaked.

"First homicides, then missing persons, then deaths from unknown causes, over the last six months."

"Okay."

He typed "F homicide," and a return. There was a brief pause, then the screen began to fill up. First was a line that said, "Doc date freq lines database headline" (I know this because it is reproduced on these papers in front of me), which was followed by information that, presumably, he understood. The only thing that made sense to me were the ends of the lines, which said such things as "Third Shooting in Commons—Neighbors Frightened." He made notes on a pad, recording what seemed to be the document numbers.

I pulled up a chair. "It seems this is going to take a while." I said. "I might as well be comfortable."

Three hours later I had a nearly complete list of homicides, deaths from unknown causes, and disappearances within the last six months, along with all known details as provided to the *Plainsman*. The police files would have been better, but also much harder to get access to.

It surprised me how much of this sort of thing there was. It would have taken quite a bit longer, but my associate had become very cooperative, even friendly, and had started pointing out ways to, as he put it, "let the machine do the work."

Still, it was quite a respectable bundle of papers. I might have had some trouble getting them home if my friend hadn't volunteered his briefcase.

But enough of that. I have the papers, and will begin to study them tomorrow.

I have spent some time going over the files from the newspaper, and discovering that it isn't quite as easy as I'd thought it would be to find what I want. I guess I was expecting to see either clear signs of Kellem's handiwork, or else clear signs of suppressed information. Unfortunately, after going through everything, I found at least a hundred cases of deaths or disappearances that could have been her work.

Perhaps she was not quite so indiscreet as she thought. Part of the problem, I suppose, is that what I'm looking at is information that has seen print, and the details that would help me are mostly those that, for one reason or another, were not included in the article. I would certainly have better luck if I could find the reporters who covered the cases, or at least their notes, but the names of the reporters are not included in the information, so I'd have to do the whole thing again. Better yet,

I suppose, would be to attempt to break into the police files, rather like the lamb sneaking into the lion's den to steal food. The notion does not appeal.

I will keep this information anyway and perhaps later I will come up with some useful way to proceed. This has been only a cursory glance; a careful study might yet produce something I can use.

Perhaps the idea was pointless to begin with. My thought had been to try to determine which crimes were going to be hung on me, so I could make some effort to protect myself. But, really, what could I do? If she is determined to destroy me in order to protect herself, than I cannot prevent it; that is the nature of our relationship, and I understood that from the beginning. She made me who I am, and she did not do so out of kindness.

And yet I'm finding my unwillingness to allow this to happen is growing, which is stupid; rather as if a stone, dropped from a cliff, had decided it was unwilling to hit the ground.

But enough. I think a visit with Jill would be very good for me just now.

Snow is falling, very heavily, and blowing about at the same time, and it is exceedingly cold. I associate snow-falls with mild, humid weather; I think this is unusual.

I am trying to remember how I made it home, and I can't do it. I walked and I ran and I stumbled, and I suppose it was painful, but I have, mercifully, no memory of it. But I find that I can sit here, and I can still operate my fingers, so I will do so.

I must do something about Jill, but it will have to wait until tomorrow; now it isn't easy for me to even sit in this chair. I wasn't certain I'd be able to work these keys, but it seems that I can, at least for now, although I seem to be getting weaker by the moment. My hands are trembling very badly, so that I'm amazed that I am not making numerous mistakes. The trembling is annoying, and it is getting worse. I tried to talk to Jim when I got home, but speaking still hurts, so I just shook my head, made my way up here, and collapsed in the chair. That hurts too, but not so much.

I must do something about Jill.

I went to see her, I think about four or five hours ago now. I entered the house, came up to her room, and just stood there. The door was open, and I wasn't being quiet, so she heard me as I came in; she was just looking at me, as if she were holding her breath to see what I'd say.

I studied her for a moment, then said, "You've redecorated."

She swallowed, it seemed to take some effort, then nodded. She didn't speak; probably couldn't.

I said, "I liked it better before." She still didn't say anything. I said, "Whose idea was this?"

When she didn't answer I said "Whose?" again, putting some snap into it.

She remained mute, like a child who doesn't know it's being addressed.

I said, "It was Don, wasn't it?" She didn't answer, so I put even more into my voice and repeated, "Wasn't it?"

At last she nodded.

I said, "I had forbidden you to see him."

She began to tremble.

"Come here," I said. After a moment she came. I pressed her into my arms. She gave a small muffled cry as the silver points of the mounting of my pendent dug into her chest. Soon she was quiet. There were footsteps, then, and I heard a door opening down the hall. Tom's head emerged from the door leading up the attic. I glared at him, but he didn't seem to notice; just nodded pleasantly to me and continued down the back stairs into the kitchen.

I took Jill by the throat and said, "Restore this room."

She nodded, just barely.

I said, "Good. I'll be back to check on you after I've settled things with Young Don."

"No," she said, very softly. "Please."

I slapped her, not very hard, and she slumped down onto the floor. "Restore this room by the time I return."

Don lived near St. Bart's, in a new, ugly, and no doubt expensive apartment building that will probably be turned into a condominium within another five years. It is two stories of greenish brick, each unit having a little porch area enclosed in an iron rail with access via French windows. They had a great deal invested in their security system.

There are a pair of pine trees flanking the walk, about ten feet in front of the doors. I got cozy with one until someone approached with a key in his hand.

A chubby, thoroughly muffled gentleman in his early thirties stepped up to the door, and I slipped out of the shadows behind him. I followed him through the first door, and stood consulting the list of residents while he unlocked the door. He stopped, looked at me, shrugged, and held the door open. I smiled a thank-you and followed him in. No words were exchanged.

Young Don lived in number 22, which I assumed would be on the second floor. I went up the stairs as if I knew for certain, while the gentleman with the key went down the hall the other way. Yes, it was on the second floor, to the right of the stairs, on the left side of the hall.

I entered without knocking first, which may have startled Young Don, because he gave a little screech just before he discharged his shotgun into my chest.

Being shot at close range by double-ought buckshot fired from a .12-gauge shotgun is like being hit by about eighteen .32 caliber bullets, all within a few inches of each other and hitting at the same time, except that I don't know of any .32 that will shoot with as much force as a shotgun has. The blast picked me up and carried me into the door with enough force that the impact of my body caused the wood to splinter behind me, so that for a moment I had the sensation of being embedded in the door, before my knees crumbled and I fell in a little heap in front of it. Of course, the wood wasn't the best.

I wish I could remember those next few seconds, because I'll bet they were interesting, but, while I have a clear memory of the feel of the door splintering behind me, the next thing I can remember is Young Don saying something I couldn't make out over the ringing in my ears, and I know that some time passed while I wasn't looking, so to speak.

I was trying to focus on what he was saying while something in my head said, "Stand up, stand up, stand up." I braced myself against the shattered door, tried to rise, failed, and tried again. I made some progress.

I heard Don say, "Jill said you'd be here."

I didn't try to speak at first; my lungs had been ruptured, and speech requires passing air in and out. I made it to a standing position, leaning against the door. Don's eyes widened. I took a ragged, experimental breath, and it seemed to work. I said, "I shall draw forth thy bones one by one ere I send thee to the Devil, that for all time thy shapeless body shall serve as a carpet for the minions of Hell."

For just a second he could only stare at me. In that time, I heard sirens approaching, and knew they were heading for us. Then Young Don worked the pump on the shotgun and pointed it at my chest again.

I laughed in his face. "You told Jill, and even told her what to do with her room, but you didn't believe it yourself, did you?"

He gave an inarticulate cry and squeezed the trigger

again, but this time I was ready; I can move very fast indeed when I have to. The blast of the shotgun faded into the approaching siren, which melted into the cry, which went on in my ears long after it had stopped in his throat.

SIX

re·per·cus·sion *n.* 1. The indirect effect, influence, or result produced by an event or action. 2. A recoil, rebounding, or reciprocal motion after impact.

AMERICAN HERITAGE DICTIONARY

Several days have passed since I was last in front of my typewriting machine, and I'm finally beginning to feel a little better. The trauma didn't hit until I tried to get up again the day after I was shot; I collapsed, and lay like a corpse until I fell asleep again several hours later. The next day, when Jim looked in on me, I was hardly able to respond to him. He seemed worried, but what could he do? More days passed in this way, though I'm not certain how many. Yesterday I felt that I might be starting to recover but I didn't want to press my luck. Today I managed to rise and, after a moment or two, stumble up to my typing room. I need to at least be doing something or I shall go mad.

I am feeling weak and lethargic, but not too bad other than that.

I think I will rest some more now, and tomorrow, or the next day at the latest, I will be about my business.

Seeing Jill I must put off for another day or two, but it is high on my list, and then—

Jim and I have had a pleasant enough chat. I told him what had happened with Jill and Don, and he has told me some of his own history, which I'd set down here but I don't remember enough of the details to make it worthwhile; it is detail that makes a story interesting.

He asked me of my own history, and I told some of it, though in no particular order; because the recollections that come bubbling forth from my memory like water from a fountain don't seem to want to emerge in any recognizable pattern; although, now that I think of it, I've been relating the day-to-day events of these past weeks very much in order; but that's merely a matter of setting down what has just happened and isn't at all the same.

For example, when I think of Laura Kellem, what I get are images of her face, or pieces of conversation that might have happened any time during the years we've known each other, or parts of the strange dreams I used to have after we'd first met. That was, I believe, while I was in my third year at University. A friend—his name escapes me—had invited me out to a tavern, and, as was our custom, after a few pints we went stalking through those areas that the painted ladies, as we called them, were known to frequent. Now, in all honesty, neither of us had ever indulged ourselves in spending time or money on these ladies. I don't know why we never did, whether it was fear of some blot that would follow us around, fear of certain diseases that clergymen and professors would hint at but never name, or merely want of courage, but it is nevertheless the case; on the other hand we both took a strange thrill in passing them by and hearing them speak to us in the cadences of their profession, voices both hard and soft, forbidding and promising.

At first, I thought Kellem was such a one, as I recall seeing her leaning with ease and confidence against the filthy wall of a boarding house in an area where no lady would venture alone; yet I realized that her ankles were decently covered, and she wore a hat, and her dress, though hanging much straighter than was fashionable (most ladies were wearing hoops), was not such as one of the painted ladies would wear, being made of some fabric of dark green with flounces, a bright yellow ribbon hanging down the front, and a small bit of white lace about the collar and the sleeves.

I was intrigued at once by the character shown on her face. I can still remember the way she appeared as if she were in command of the street, as if no one could possibly question her right to be there or make any insinuations about her, much less accost her unpleasantly; and there was, at the same time, a glint of humor in her eyes as if all she saw amused her. I did not then understand it, though I do now.

My first thought was that she had a far more interesting face than Prudence, to whom I had recently become engaged; my second was to reproach myself for thinking such things. It was because of that, no doubt, that, as we walked by, I sent her a look of scorn, as if she were, indeed, what I had first taken her for. To this day I don't know if that look annoyed her or amused her, but, at all events, she called out to me as I went by.

"Young man," she said, in a voice at once melodious and sharp, like the timbre of a flute without the breathiness.

We stopped, my friend and I (his name was Richard, I now recall), stopped and looked at each other, then at her. I bowed slightly and said, "Yes, madam?"

For a moment she just stared at me, smiling a secret smile, and the moment grew to the point where I became uncomfortable, although I found her eyes fascinating, as if they had a mysterious pull that promised rapture beyond the limitations of earthly lust or heavenly love. At last she said, "I have become lost, I'm afraid. Would you mind escorting me home?"

Richard and I looked at each other once more, but, after all, she was clearly a lady; how could we refuse? We placed her between us, and she took my arm and we began walking in I know not what direction. Nor, now that I think of it, do I know what became of Richard that night; I do not believe it has ever occurred to me until now to wonder how she managed to get me to her rooms alone without giving either Richard or me any suspicion that anything out of the ordinary was happening. I don't believe that Richard ever even spoke of the event; it was as if he'd forgotten it had happened; and I certainly never brought it up. But Richard, and, for that matter, Prudence, all begin to fade from memory at about that same time, so I cannot be certain.

All in all, it was a simple and elegant seduction. I've done it many times, and perhaps as well, though certainly never better.

I have discovered a place called Flannery's, located on Terrace, near Fullerton, which is right on the edge of Little Philly. They have a strip bar in front, the sort where the strippers are forty-year-old women wearing caked-on makeup in hopes that a myopic drunk will think they're college girls and tip accordingly. The drink prices are high, but not as high as the bars where the college girls do "lingerie shows."

In any case, they have a back room where one can play poker. It is a typical arrangement: the house supplies the dealer, takes five percent of each pot, makes sure there's a waitress around, and other than that the players are left alone. I was down to a couple of hundred dollars when I started; I left with a little less than three thousand.

Playing cards isn't the easiest way I know to get the money I need to make life comfortable, but I think it is my favorite. I'm careful at first; staying with small pots and folding if I'm not sure. But after about an hour I get so I can pretty well see who has what, and by the time I've been playing with the same people for two hours, I cannot be fooled, or "bluffed" in the parlance of the game.

An experienced dealer can tell at once if there is so much as one card missing from the deck, but after he's been sitting with me for a couple of hours I can stop worrying. Yet even though I cannot be bluffed, and even though I might have a nine of diamonds waiting to be slipped in where needed, still, every hand is different and I never know what kind of luck I am going to have. Or, to put it another way, I know I'm not going to lose, but I enjoy the process of discovering exactly how I'm going to win.

One of the waitresses, a tall redhead with an odd trace of Latino in her face, started noticing me after a few hours and being especially nice; I guess she was watching the pile of money in front of me grow. By this time the bar was closed, and there were only two waitresses working the four tables of card players. I tipped her well, and returned some of her inane banter, but I realized, as I was beginning to think about leaving, that I had no interest in her at all.

There were ugly looks when I left; it's that sort of place; and the waitress seemed disappointed, but I left the bar alone. I walked through the heart of Little Philly, which is an area I'd heard talk about, and noticed from newspaper accounts as being dangerous. It seemed quiet enough to me; there were more police cruisers than anything else, and it had none of the atmosphere of danger that I remember from the Lower East Side of New York, or certain parts of Soho. I guess everything is relative.

The rats still played in the sewers, though, and there

were a few stray cats who paced me, and a few dogs who howled and ran off. People talk about how peaceful the countryside is, or the deep woods, or the mountains, or the lakes. Maybe so. But there is a certain kind of peace that you find in the middle of a city when you are the only one on the street, and you can hear your footsteps echo on the dry pavement, and the smell of petrol and exhaust is only the faint lingering reminder of what the place is like when it is alive.

The walk was not unpleasant; there was no moon to contend with the stars that were visible through the glow of the streetlights and I was not cold. I expect February to be the coldest month, but I'm told that in Ohio January is usually the worst. February still has a firm grip, but she's so confident that she doesn't mind letting the thermometer climb just a little, knowing she can send it back down whenever she wants to. This is such an evening, and I can even imagine that someday the snow will melt, and the pavement will begin to sprout once more. I wonder if I will see the spring.

I regret leaving without that waitress. I am still feeling weak, and very tired.

The nights are getting shorter.

It is time for me to sleep.

This evening seems to be shaping up very nicely indeed. There is a low cloud cover, a breeze that is almost warm, and no moon. The breeze carries with it the least hint of news from the north, suggesting colder weather to come, but I think it is lying; I believe we will have another day or two of relative warmth before the next murderous cold wave hits. In either case, tonight is pleasant enough.

I dreamed about Susan, and woke up seeing her face.

This is no good. While it has been very nice spending time with her, I cannot afford, especialy now, to

To what? I don't know how to complete that sentence.

Well, it doesn't matter. It is time to pay Jill the visit I owe her; for I have no doubt that she has not done what I commanded her to, and probably thinks me out of her life. I will correct this misapprehension, and I will not allow myself to be distracted by her roommate.

It is time to be about it.

I'm a little puzzled by

Oh, this is too amusing for words. Between the previous line and this one has been about five minutes of laughter, bordering on the hysterical at times. Jim came in and looked at me, but I just shook my head and didn't say anything, so he shrugged and went away. The best jokes, I think, are those played by Lady Fate, and she has just performed a fine one. Let me set this down so that, if sometime later I come to read it, I will be able to savor the humor in all its grandeur.

Jill wasn't home when I got there, and, as I'd expected, she hadn't made the changes in her room that I had ordered. I seethed for a moment, then shrugged and went down the hall to say a quick hello to Susan, who was standing in the bathroom, naked, with the door open, brushing her hair. I watched her for a moment, admiring the curve of her back and the set of her shoulders, then went up and stood next to her.

She jumped, but only a little.

"I didn't mean to startle you," I said.

"You move like a cat."

"Miaow."

She gave me one of her extravagant smiles, then looked puzzled and said, "How did you get in?"

"I picked the lock, broke a window, and came down the chimney."

"Oh, the usual."

"Right."

"Vivian always said that a man who couldn't surprise you is a waste of time."

"Surprise, surprise," I said.

She smiled into my eyes. "Jill isn't here, you know."

"I know. You are."

"Yes," she said, "I am," and came into my arms. Some time later I carried her into the bedroom.

I don't know why I bother making promises to myself when I know I can't keep them.

I was still there some hours later when her eyelids fluttered open. She curled up next to me and said, "You're dressed." Her voice was a little hoarse.

I traced my initials on her side and said, "Yes."

"Is Jill home?"

"I heard her come in about an hour ago."

"What did she say?"

"The door was closed; I doubt she knows I'm here."

"You didn't talk to her?"

"No. Not yet."

"Mmmmm."

She stretched a little in happy contentment as I watched. I took my feelings out and examined them; surprised, not at the state she was in, but at my own pride in having brought her there. I said, "What do you think of Jill's room?"

"Mmmmm. It's her room. She hasn't gotten evangelical on me, so I don't really care. She did try to put those things all over the house, but I put my foot down. I live here, too."

"Indeed. But isn't that what you meant before about claiming territory?"

"Yes," she said brightly. "But she didn't succeed."

"I should imagine," I said, "that many women dislike you."

She looked hurt, and for a moment I was afraid she was going to cry. "Hey," I said. "I didn't mean—"

She shook her head and smiled as if sharing a joke with herself. "Not as many as all that," she said. Then she was serious again. "But I don't understand why." This was said very softly.

I realized I'd hit a sore spot, and I didn't know what to say. "You don't? Women are so often territorial when it comes to men, and you—"

"Oh, come now, Jonathan. I respect boundaries as much as anyone."

"But you said—"

"It is simply a matter of establishing them in my home."

"I think I understand."

"I don't make it a practice to, what is the word? Poach. I think I've heard it called that, as if men were some sort of game that could only be hunted in season and in certain places. What a revolting idea."

"Well—"

"But if someone has a lover, I don't interfere."

"Good idea."

"So why is that so many women feel threatened by me?"

"You're asking me? I have no idea." I looked around for a way to change the subject, feeling a little uncomfortable with this one. I said, "Did the sudden change surprise you?"

"What change?"

"In Jill."

"Oh. Yes, I suppose it did," she said reflectively, "but it shouldn't have. She hasn't been very happy lately, and the thing with Don was the last straw, I think. She hasn't been willing to talk about it. I ought to have predicted either this or drugs, and this is better."

"What thing with Don?"

"Didn't you hear?"

"No."

She shook her head and I think was going to tell me, but then she yawned and suddenly looked very sleepy, and she dozed off before she got around to it. I picked up my coat and went over to Jill's room. I waited just outside of it. Presently, Jill came out, looking vaguely confused. She saw me, and the shock grew in her eyes. She opened her mouth and took in a breath. I clapped my hand over her mouth. "Don't wake up Susan," I said. "She's sleeping."

She did her best to wake her up anyway, but I had her in a firm grip. She stank, horribly, so that I almost gagged from being next to her, but I forced myself to endure it long enough to strip off everything she was wearing. I couldn't help but laugh. "All of that nonsense in your room, and only the stench on your person? One might doubt your sincerity. Or your intelligence, at any rate." This only made her struggle harder; I had to choke her almost unconscious, but at last it was done. I dragged her to the bathroom and turned on the cold water, then pulled the knob for the shower. She continued to struggle the entire time. When the smell was gone I took her from the shower, pushed her against the wall and held her until she stopped struggling.

I finally took my hand away from her mouth and told her exactly what she was going to do. She nodded her agreement, but when I released her she took a step, then collapsed to the floor and began to tremble violently, as if she were having some sort of seizure. I knew she wasn't diabetic, but perhaps she was an epileptic; if so, I didn't know what to do except to try to keep her from hurting herself in her thrashings; and it seemed reasonable that I ought to try to keep her warm.

I wrapped her in a towel and carried her down to the couch, where she lay twisting and jerking violently for a long time, until she gradually settled down to shivering. Her face went through the most amazing contortions, as if she were trying to disown her tongue. I put an Afghan comforter over her, and then, when she kept trembling, I added a few coats. After about an hour, she abruptly stopped, broke into a sweat, and lay perfectly still in a sleep from which I could not wake her. I checked her breathing, which seemed fine, and her pulse, which was racing at first, but gradually settled down.

Not knowing what else to do I went home and came up to my typing room, put a fresh piece of paper in the machine and began to hit the keys. It was only then that I noticed that my right hand itched the way skin does when it is repairing itself, though I had not noticed being hurt. I looked, and saw the traces of the damage still there in my palm, which is when I stopped and, as I said, laughed almost hysterically for a while. I couldn't help it.

Apparently, while attempting to escape my muffling, Jill had bitten my hand hard enough to draw blood.

SEVEN

Kellem spoke to me of dreams, and just yesterday I made reference to the dreams I used to have when I first knew her, and now I've had another one. Of course, I always dream, and I often remember what I dream, but I'm not speaking now about vague impressions filtered from memories, fears, and the sights and sounds that infiltrate the benumbed senses of the sleeper to invade his thoughts without waking him; I am speaking of a dream that comes with all the power of significance, and tells you what you did not know before—or would tell you if you knew how to interpret it. And then there are dreams that not only inform, but are part of the process of change— dreams that visit the world as it visits the sleeper. But we don't really believe in those, do we?

I dreamt of Jill, naturally. Oh, certainly there was enough of the confusing dream landscape, as there always is; Kellem appeared now and then, doing what she does in life; but for the most part it was Jill, looking at

me with varying expressions of horror, tenderness, wist-
fulness, defiance, and even lust—more expression, in
fact, than I'd ever seen on her face in the real world, so
I think my imagination supplied a great deal of it.

In my dream we were walking around and around
some object set in the middle of a room, like a large chair,
although I don't think I was ever certain what the object
was. We were playing a silly game of can't-catch-me, but
there was great urgency to the game, for all that we were,
at times, laughing as we played. Then, without a resolution to the game, I was standing in front of her, holding
both of her shoulders and saying, "Have you done what
I ordered you to?"

She tried to look away from me, but I would not let
her; in the dream, the force of my will was tangible, and
very, very strong. In the end she shuddered and collapsed
into some poorly defined small, furry thing, which scam-
pered off to go fetch something or other in response to
my command.

I awoke some time after this, knowing at once that
the next time I saw her she would have fulfilled my
wishes, and taken by a strong desire to set this dream
down on paper before I forgot it; I don't think I've ever
had a dream like this before; I don't think the circumstances which caused it to be have ever come up before.

I will visit Jill now, and discover if I have been
deceived.

She was sitting quietly on her bed, her back resting on the
wall. Her room had been partially restored to its former
splendor—that is, the additions had been removed, but
the artwork had not been put up again. She was wearing
a white dressing gown, and I had the impression that she
had been sitting there, just like that, for hours, maybe
days.

I came in and shut the door behind me. She turned

her head slowly, but her face betrayed no expression. I looked at her for just a moment, then she stirred herself—it seemed to take some effort—and rose from the bed. She stood before me, unbuttoned her dressing gown, let it fall to the floor, and waited.

Afterward I covered her up and left her sleeping deeply.

I went down the stairs and found Susan sitting on the couch, her feet up. She was wearing another light blue tank top and a green printed skirt. She said, "I never heard you come in."

"I've been upstairs seeing Jill," I said.

She put down her reading matter, which seemed to be a textbook, and said, "Is she any better?"

"No. Well, maybe. Her room looks better."

"Yes. That didn't last long. I wonder what she'll find next."

"She's sleeping now, at any rate."

"I think Don's death hit her pretty hard."

"Apparently."

"She needs to come out of it, though."

"Have you ever lost anyone close?"

She nodded slowly. "Yes. My friend Vivian."

"Oh. I hadn't realized."

"It's been almost two years, now. I could say a drunk crashed into her, and it would be true, but she was pretty loaded herself."

"I'm sorry."

"Yes." Her face is amazing. Even when she was holding back any expression I could almost read her feelings like words on a page. I can't help comparing her to Jill, whose face is dead, or Kellem, who hardly ever lets her feelings show. Except anger. Kellem has always been willing to show anger.

I studied Susan's face and said, "But you've recovered from her death, I think."

"Yes."

"How?

She considered this. "Vivian was one of the wittiest people I've ever known, and one of the wisest. I wrote down everything I could remember that she'd ever said, and every once in a while I read through things, and I quote her from time to time."

"You're keeping her with you."

"Yes."

"You are very beautiful."

She stood up and I held her, but that is all I did, then, because it wouldn't have felt right to do more. I did kiss her once, lightly, as I was leaving. She said, "Your lips are always so cold."

I started to say "Like my heart," but I didn't, for fear that she might believe me.

An altogether splendid evening; although, consequently and ironically, there is little to say about it. But it has gotten me back to work on the typewriting machine. I woke up completely recovered, and, in fact, feeling rather better than I have in some time. I took the opportunity to visit Susan, who was looking slightly wan but seemed to be in fine spirits.

After checking on Jill, who was doing better, we went off and saw a play at a little private theater in the Tunnel. The theater is called the Clubhouse, and the play itself was a fairly recent work by someone I'd never heard of that was about three generations of women and concerned itself with insanity, spelling bees, and all manner of subjects in between. It was both written and performed with a good deal of humor and genuine pathos.

Susan laughed up until the end, when she cried, and then I took her home, kissed her hand at the door and bid good evening to her surprised, slightly disappointed, but seemingly charmed countenance.

Even the weather has conspired to make this a pleasant night, because, although it was cold, it was also a
beautiful clear night without wind, and the sliver of
moon was sharp and fine before she fell into the western
skyline. The lack of wind is also serving to keep this room
more snug than usual.

I feel very much like having a nice chat with Jim, so
I believe that I will.

Kellem has started the game.

My spirits have improved, now that it has begun; I
still don't know precisely what she has planned, but at
least I know she has started. I am more relaxed than I
have been in quite some time.

I had came out of the shower; I was naked except for
a towel wrapped around my head; when Jim walked up
to me silently and said without preamble, "The police
were here today."

I pulled the towel away and looked at him. He was
staring at the steamy bathroom over my shoulder. "Ah,"
I said.

"It was about nine o'clock this morning. They
knocked on the door, then broke it down."

"You didn't let them in?"

Jim, apparently, didn't think that was very funny.
"There were seven of them, six in uniform and one in
plainclothes."

"How were they armed?"

"Two had shotguns, the rest weren't carrying anything."

"I don't like shotguns."

"I know."

"In the future, don't allow them in the house."

He barely smiled.

I said, "Did they search?"

"Oh, yes. Up one side and down the other. They were at it a good five, six hours."

"What did they find?"

"Well, they didn't find you."

"I'd sort of figured that out already. What *did* they find?"

He almost laughed. "Some dirty laundry."

"Did they take it?"

"I'm afraid so."

I tried to remember what I'd left out so I could determine how annoyed I ought to be. When a place has a nice hideyhole like this one does, I tend to make sure everything is there before I sleep (including these papers, by the way). I remembered that there was a nice silk shirt that I'd miss, but everything else was easily replaceable. If they had come two days earlier, they'd have found a week's worth of dirty laundry. "Much joy may it bring them," I said. "What did they say?"

"Most of what they talked about didn't have anything to do with their search, and I don't really care to repeat it."

"Ah."

"But they did learn that someone had been staying here, both from the laundry and from the burned candles and the ash in the fireplace."

"Did they check for fingerprints?"

"All over."

"Okay. They won't match anything anyway."

He looked startled. "You've never had your prints taken before?"

"Now, Jim," I said. "You know I try to stay on the right side of the law."

That time he laughed, though I think it was a bit forced. "What do you think they were after?"

"After?" I said. "Me, of course."

"Well, yes, but why?"

"With that many of them? They probably think I'm dangerous. I would imagine Kellem arranged this in hopes they'd find me while I slept."

He shook his head. "I thought you said she wouldn't want that."

"Well, yes, but apparently I was wrong. Unless you think it's coincidence."

"Not hardly," said Jim. "What are you going to do about it?"

"After this," I said. "I'm going to pick up my dirty laundry."

I got dressed in what used to be the master bedroom. This has become a habit with me, to stand in front of the fireplace, dry myself off as if there were a fire going, then go over to the dressing room attached to it and put on whatever I've chosen to wear that day. Today, for the record, I'm wearing black zip boots, black pants, a navy blue turtleneck shirt and a brown corduroy sports coat. And my pendant, of course; I've had it for a long, long time, and it has become a sort of good-luck piece for me, although I'm not really superstitious. (I used to be very superstitious, but then I learned it was bad luck. A little joke there, Jim). It was Kellem who gave me the pendant, now that I think of it. She said it reminded her of me. I didn't know what she meant, and, come to that, I still don't; she probably just said it for effect. In any case, while I don't pay a great deal of attention to my dress, and I tend to leave almost everything when I move, I do like to look presentable. The shoes, by the way, haven't quite broken in and they hurt just a little.

It's time to get serious about this; the game's afoot, Watson, I need you. I'm going to take those papers out again and go through them once more.

Completely frustrated. I've been able to eliminate a few cases, but not enough to help. It seems Kellem ought to have been polite enough to leave some sort of signs on her kills. Is this what she calls being obvious? I suppose I could tell her that she's overreacting, but the last time I tried to talk to her it didn't work out so well.

I am tempted to try to get into the police station and go through their files, but that does seem like asking for trouble. What if they have a description of me, and I'm spotted the instant I go in?

I would love to be able to talk to Susan about this. Not that I think she could help, but it would be pleasant to be able to unload my frustration on her. Still, there's always Jim, who has been very patient with me.

I'm not sure what to do next. Ignore everything and hope something comes up? Wait for inspiration to strike? Track down Kellem at her lair? And then what? At least I no longer have to worry about Jill or Don.

Although, now that I think of it, how did Don know what to do? Even if he'd watched a few movies and read a few novels, his knowledge seemed far too complete. There's a mystery there. I might have been too hasty with him; although it is certainly too late to worry about that now. But perhaps I ought to try to find the source of his knowledge. At any rate, that will give me something to do.

I've just come back from spending a few hours visiting our neighbor, Bill. I met him and his infuriating dog again as I was leaving the house, and, once again, the dog nearly went berserk. Bill apologized, and we spoke, and he renewed his offer, and this time I accepted. Their house is about as different from Jim's as you can imagine for two houses in the same neighborhood. It is from the 1950's, a style I detest, with low ceilings and space conservation everywhere; although when the forced-air heating system started up I began to see the virtues. It is very simply decorated, mostly with books. I was pleased to see a good number of old, leather-bound editions of Dickens and Hawthorne and such.

The dog wouldn't settle down, so they put it out in the fenced-in backyard, and showered me with apologies about which I was quite gracious.

His wife's name is Dorothy (I didn't ask her if she was from Kansas, although I was tempted), and she's a bright, slightly dumpy middle-aged woman with salt-and-pepper hair. They tried to feed me and I declined, eventually accepting half a cup of coffee.

We spoke about the college, and he mentioned that he had a new project.

"What's that?" I said.

"It's called the Swaggart Study."

"From Jimmy Swaggart?"

"No, no, Don Swaggart."

I kept my face impassive. "I don't believe I've heard of him."

"He's the guy who started the project, over in Sociology."

"Oh."

"He died recently, and he was pretty much the main force behind it, so we decided to keep it going in his honor and name it after him."

"That was thoughtful. An older fellow?"

"No, quite young. He was killed. Some sort of break-in at his house."

"Really? A shame. Did you know him?"

Bill nodded. "Yes. Very well, in fact."

"I'm sorry," I said.

"It was a shock. It's hard to get to be my age without having a close friend die unexpectedly like that, but I've managed."

"I've never gotten used to it myself," I said.

He nodded, then laughed a little. "I still don't quite

believe it. I mean, I've read Spider Robinson; people don't *really* die. Not *dead* dead."

"Who?"

"Never mind."

Dorothy offered me some Rondele on crackers which I declined, and then she asked if I had any children.

"No. Do you?" Which was the cue for them to get the pictures out. Lord! They even had a son in the army, stationed in Germany; it was the kind of photograph that makes you think the kid is an officer if you don't know insignia. They also had a daughter who, judging from her graduation picture, was not unattractive. I started to ask about her, then changed my mind.

The conversation drifted after that. Bill brought up Young Don once or twice more, but I had nothing to say about him, and we eventually worked our way to a discussion of crime in general. I was able to keep a straight face while agreeing with most of what they said.

Then Dorothy said, "The police were over at the house across the street today."

"Really?" said Bill and I at the same time.

She nodded. "I went out and asked one of the officers what was going on, and he ordered me back in the house."

"It must have been serious, then," I said.

Bill nodded. "That's the real problem with empty houses; you never know who might move in, unofficially."

"Indeed," I said. "That is very true."

A long day today. I went back to see Jill, hoping she might be able to tell me where Young Don got his great ideas. I opened up her door and went in, and found the place full of flowers, a tray next to the bed, a teapot and cup on the tray, and Jill lying sound asleep. Someone had evidently been taking care of her.

I tried to wake her up, but she only moaned a little and, if anything, fell deeper into unconsciousness. Not knowing what else to do, I turned to go, and found Susan in the doorway, looking at me with an expression that seemed puzzled and not entirely happy. I held my smile until I should know what she was about. She didn't waste any time telling me.

"What have you been doing to Jill?" she said. She looked right at me, her voice and expression without fear or compromise, and I felt the way I suppose the lion feels when confronted by his trainer with whip and chair.

Yet, despite the horrible plunging sensation in my chest, and the odd tingling at the bottoms of my feet and in my palms, I determined not to give up anything more than necessary. I said, "What do you mean?"

"Jill," she said, "has been lying here all day, hardly waking up for more than five or ten minutes, and she's been calling your name and moaning."

"Perhaps," I said, "she misses me."

"She's been moaning 'no, Jack, please don't.' Does that sound like she misses you?"

It came to me that I'd been hearing those very words, in her voice, while I was sleeping. In my dreams I had thought it slightly amusing; now I did not. I groped for a reply, and finally settled on asking "Could she mean, please don't go?"

"I think not," said Susan, biting out the words one at a time. She was still looking at me in a manner that was nearly accusing.

My temper began to rise, and I had an almost over-powering urge to take Susan right then, whatever her desires; almost overpowering, not quite. I don't know what it was that held me back, but for a moment things hung in the balance, and in that time I think Susan saw a side of me I had not intended to show her. At any rate, she took a step backward and watched me the way one might watch a dog whose disposition has not been ascertained.

But this time, the dog only bristled a little. I regained composure, and Susan regained her puzzled look, and she seemed to shake herself as if she weren't quite certain what it was that she almost saw.

I said, "I can hardly be responsible for her delirium. Have you consulted a doctor?"

She frowned. "No. Do you think I should?"

"Does she seem sick?"

"Look at her."

"Well, then perhaps calling a doctor would be more productive than accusing me of I know not what crimes against your roommate."

She took a couple of deep breaths, then nodded. "I'm sorry I snapped at you," she said. "I'm worried about Jill."

"Yes. As far as I can tell, you have reason to be."

"Then should I—?"

"Yes. If she's still like this tomorrow, I'd call a doctor."

"Tomorrow?"

"You could do it now, if you're worried, but I should give it another day."

She nodded, and I think what had really been bothering her was that she hadn't quite known what to do with a roommate as sick as Jill apparently was, nor had she had anyone to ask. "Wait another day, you think?" she said again, as if for more reassurance.

"That's what I'd do, unless she seems to be getting worse."

"Okay," she said, relaxing as the decision was made. "That's what I'll do."

Now I frowned. "You look a little pale yourself. Have you eaten today?"

She blinked, as if it were a question that would never have occurred to her. "You know, I don't believe I have. Are you hungry?"

"No, but I can keep you company. Where shall we go?"

She smiled, and she was the Susan I knew again. "Out," she said, swinging her arms.

"Shhhh. Don't wake patient."

She lowered her voice, but said, "I doubt that I could."

I led the way. As we locked the front door behind us, she said, "How *do* you keep getting in without my knowing it? Did Jill give you a key without mentioning it to me?"

"Trade secret," I said.

"What trade is that? Cat burglar?"

"Yes, although I prefer the technical term."

"What's that?"

"Music promoter."

She laughed. "You aren't really a promoter, are you?"

"No, I'm afraid not. If I were, I'd give you a contract."

"I don't doubt that a bit," she said.

The wind was fierce, so I sheltered her with my body. It's funny, but there is a kind of intimacy that vanishes along with one's clothes, and that can sometimes become stronger as more layers are added. Walking beneath the new moon, huddling against the wind and the occasional streetlights, I almost felt as if we were a single person, intertwining our emotions with our hair, her breath steaming around our heads.

She said, "There's something fey about you, you know."

"Fey?" I laughed. "I've never been called fey before."

"You haven't? I'm surprised."

"I must say I prefer it to some of the things I have been called."

She chuckled into the collar of my coat. "Don't tell me," she said, her voice muffled. The top of her head looked very charming that way.

"I shan't."

We found a restaurant called the Nawlins, which was a storefront with too many tables and not enough waiters for the space, and I bought her some shrimp Creole and a beer, which she seemed to thoroughly enjoy. After the beer she switched to coffee, and I joined her with my usual half-cup. She seemed to think that was funny.

She asked about my love life, which threw me for a bit, but I ended up telling her about Kellem, although in general terms and not by name. Susan thinks Kellem is very frightened, and wants a man to make her feel secure, but is afraid to trust anyone enough to make a difference. I almost laughed at this, and then I began wondering if there wasn't some truth in it. I still wonder.

We drifted onto other subjects, and I cannot for the life of me remember what we talked about, but we suddenly noticed that everyone else had left and the busboy, a college-aged kid who'd gone to the Art Garfunkel school of hair fashion, was giving us significant looks. I left an extra tip for his trouble and helped Susan with her coat.

"Back home?" I said. "Or is there somewhere else worth going?"

"I wish it were summer so we could walk along the lakeshore."

"We can anyway. Stand on the rocks and watch the waves crash while the wind—"

"Freezes our cute little behinds off. No thanks."

"You have no trace of romance in you," I said.

She smiled at me. "Wanna bet?"

"Right. Home then."

We made it in spite of the powdered snow that the wind threw into our faces, though my hands were thoroughly chilled. When we got inside, I said, "You're going to have to warm me up."

"Let's check on Jill, first," she said.

"All right."

So we did, and decided that she seemed to be breathing a little easier, though she still didn't wake up. Then I took Susan's hand and led her into the bedroom.

All right, yeah, she did have some romance in her, after all.

EIGHT

troub·le *n.* 1. A state of distress, affliction, danger, or need. Often used in the phrase *in trouble.* 2. Something that contributes to such a state; a difficulty or problem: *One trouble after another delayed the job.* 3. Exertion; effort; pains. 4. A condition of pain, disease, or malfunction: *heart trouble.* —*v.* **troubled, -ling, -les.** —*tr.* 1. To agitate; stir up. 2. To afflict with pain or discomfort. 3. To cause distress or confusion in.

AMERICAN HERITAGE DICTIONARY

I had finished typing up the tale of yesterday and was preparing for sleep when Jim came up and told me that Kellem had been over looking for me. I cursed under my breath and said, "Did she say what she wanted?"

"No," said Jim. "She didn't seem upset that you weren't here."

"Did you invite her in?"

He nodded. "She insisted."

"What did she do?"

"Looked around a little, complimented me on the woodwork and the fixtures."

"That's all?"

"Yes."

Jim didn't seem happy about it, but, come to that, he has been very moody since the visit of the police; I don't know if he is worried on my behalf, or upset about having his home invaded. Perhaps some of each. I would like to go down and make a fire, but I don't dare; the smoke might be seen. Instead, I will spend some more time going over the newspaper articles, useless as I now think that will be.

I wish I could find a way to learn or deduce what Kellem has done that worries her so. If I could find a means of protecting her that would not cost my life, I could perhaps convince her to accept it, in spite of what happened the last time I tried to speak to her.

And why shouldn't she be willing to grant me my life, if she can do so at no cost or danger to herself? It isn't as if she has never cared for me. Years ago, we used to spend a great deal of time together—more than she would have had to. But I was utterly taken with her, and I think she enjoyed being worshiped as intensely as I worshiped her.

We would spend hour after hour just walking and talking, me eagerly asking questions about her life and the ways of her world, and she would take me to the theater and hold forth on philosophy or tell me stories of people she had known. Her decision to leave London, and, in fact, the British Isles, came a few weeks before the battle of Atbara, and she helped me through that first horrible winter crossing of the Channel.

On the Continent, however, I at once fell in love with the European railways, and in this way we traveled together for some months or years. I took her to my boyhood home, to which I had not returned in quite some time, and she showed me Paris. I remember very little of that city, except that I can recall thinking that it would be wonderful if there weren't so many Frenchmen there. But mostly I was still involved with her, and I doted on her every word and action.

I remember her saying, "Things aren't like they once were, and for that you ought to be grateful. For years, for decades, I would spend my time in the shadows of the great cities, only occasionally daring to venture out into the light of society, and then never for long. Now we can walk the streets, shop, visit the theater, and it is as if we exist within a shelter. The old terrors that hardened me and trained me are gone, and I wonder if you will ever appreciate the life you enjoy."

I can remember looking at her as she spoke; she wore a dark tailored green dress, very tight at the waist, belted, with a long fur around her neck like a scarf. The hemline came above her ankles, but she wore very trim black boots with pointed toes and square heels. I wore a long coat with eight-inch fur cuffs, a large fur collar, a white silk cravat, and a top hat, I believe. She had picked the clothes out for me with care that felt loving to my befogged brain, and perhaps it was.

I remember these things, and what she said, and that it was late autumn, and that we were in Paris, yet I cannot remember what the streets looked like, or if we were sitting, standing, or walking. No, now that I think of it, I believe we were walking through a park and there was no one around, and no sounds except our speech, the faint clop and squeak of someone's private coach a few hundred feet away, the songs of night birds, and, very faint, the titter of the rats of Paris, whose conversation never altered. The moon shone very bright on Laura's face, giving it an odd yellowish tint and highlighting her arching eyebrows and deep-set, narrow eyes that were always so cold and blue.

I considered her words, and tried to imagine what it would have been like living in the times she spoke of, and at last I asked, "What changed?"

"Time," she said. "The advent of this modern, scientific age." There was more than just a hint of derision in her voice as she spoke.

"Will it last?"

"I believe it is very nearly ending already, more's the pity."

"What makes you think so?"

"You haven't been keeping up with contemporary literature."

"I never do, Laura," I said. "I like older work."

"Then you're a fool," she snapped. "There is no better way to keep track of the thinking of men, and if you don't know what men are thinking, you don't know what precautions to take."

"Is that why we left England?"

"It was time to leave the English-speaking world for a while. I don't know for how long."

"Fortunately, you like French novels, too."

"Yes, but French drama is impossible."

"Still—"

"Yes. I'll have a pretty good guess when it's time to leave. But will you?"

"I? Won't you be—"

"Not forever, Agyar János. How well can you read French?"

"Well enough."

"Good. That may save you."

"I'm glad you care what happens to me."

She laughed, which for some reason I took as reassurance, although I cannot now imagine why I did.

We create our own omens, I think, and then mystify ourselves trying to understand their significance. That is, it feels very like an omen that this conversation has just now returned to me, in Technicolor and Dolby stereo, but I cannot imagine what it portends.

Jim keeps trying to understand what Kellem is up to. For that matter, so do I. He said, "I can't figure out what she was hoping to get from having all of those policemen look at the house, or the reason for her visit."

"I can't either," I said. "If I knew what she was trying to do, I could . . ."

"You could what?" he said.

"I don't know. I'd feel better."

"Well, it doesn't make sense; no sir, it just doesn't. If she wanted them to find you, she could have made you be more obvious, right?"

"Right."

"And if she didn't, what was the point?"

"To scare me, maybe; to get me to make a mistake."

"Why go through all that to get you to make a mistake, when she could just tell you what mistake to make, and you'd have to do it?"

"There's that," I said.

"Maybe she isn't after what you think she's after."

"Maybe."

His eyes focused on me for a moment before shifting away again. "You look, I don't know, younger than you did."

"It's what comes of a healthy life-style. You could take a lesson from it."

"I surely could, yessir."

We sat for a moment in a stillness that suddenly made me uncomfortable. I said, "I wish I could start a fire."

"There's no more wood in here; you'd have to bring it in from the carriage house."

"Maybe I will. Want to toast marshmallows?"

That pulled a laugh from him, albeit a small one. "Sure. Then what would we do with them?"

"Nothing," I said. "I just enjoy watching them burn."

The storm has ended, and I am shivering with cold; my fingers are tingling as they return to life. Perhaps it is a torture I inflict on myself to type while my hands are in this condition. If so, it is stupid. I will wait for a few minutes, then resume.

There. That is better. I don't know if I've mentioned before that the windows in the typing room (there are two, one facing west and the other facing south) are boarded up. They are covered by thin plywood strips, and not perfectly, so just at the moment, with all the clouds having dissipated as suddenly as they appeared, I am receiving some light from the half-moon, which is cutting through the slats and making a sharp white image across the keys as she sinks. The weather has warmed slightly, but it is still cold, or my fingers should have warmed up sooner; but I am not inclined to start yet another fire and warm myself up thoroughly. I wonder if it would be possible to get the furnace going; it is a hot-water radiator furnace and newer than one would suppose. Does this kind of furnace produce visible smoke? Probably.

I felt that Jill had recovered enough that I could go and see her again, although I made yet another firm resolve to stay away from Susan. She has a very active life, and I didn't want her to come down with some strange illness that matched Jill's, and would cause doctors to start paying attention. In a general sense, doctors are the least of my worries, but why should I take unnecessary chances? And I don't really want to make Susan start missing classes.

So I said to myself.

Heh.

I took myself to the big white house with blue lights in the attic, I entered, and found the living room empty and the inside lights off. I climbed the stairs, nodded to the saint pictured in the stained glass, and came to Jill's door, which I opened. She was awake, sitting up in bed, I think just staring off into space. She showed no surprise when I came in; just dropped her eyes, then unbuttoned the top of her nightgown, then looked at the wall in front of her and waited.

I looked at her carefully. She was still pale, as from illness, and had unhealthy-looking circles under her eyes. Her hand, outside of her blanket, seemed to tremble slightly. I shook my head, which attracted her attention enough that her eyes returned to me; she looked puzzled.

"Not tonight," I said. "I have a headache."

She frowned and shook her head slightly, not understanding. I sighed. "Just rest," I said. "Eat a lot. You need to recover."

"But you—?" she said, her voice barely above a whisper.

"I can wait. I don't want to kill you, child."

"Why not?"

"You are of no use to me dead."

"Oh." Her lips formed the word, but I heard no sound.

I thought I would say hello to Susan, so I went over and tapped softly on her bedroom door. She called for me to come in. She was lying in bed, hands clasped behind her head. The bedclothes were down by her waist and she wore nothing. She greeted me with words I cannot now recall. Then, I suppose seeing some expression on my face, she said, "What is it, Jonathan?"

"There is a scent in this room," I said. "A cologne that I do not recognize."

"Oh, yes, that is Jennifer's."

"Jennifer?"

"A friend."

There was a burgundy-colored button-up blouse draped over a chair. Susan would not wear burgundy. It came to me that the last time I'd been in her room, there had been a pink sweater hanging from one of the knobs of the closet door, and she wouldn't wear pink, either.

"What is it, Jonathan?"

And, beyond the perfume, there was the unmistakable odor of sex in the room. Recent sex.

I said, "What did you say your friend's name is?"

"Jennifer." And yes, it was there in the way she said her friend's name, too. Perhaps everyone else called her Jenny, but Susan had needed her version, one that she could say sleepily, while holding her in the warm afterglow of love.

I said, "I just wanted to say hello."

"Well, hello," she said brightly.

I smiled, keeping my feelings off my face, and closed the door. I went back into Jill's room. She hadn't moved. I took her shoulders in my hands; it came to me, as if from somewhere outside of myself, that if I let myself begin I would kill her; so I threw her back onto the bed. I heard something like a sob escape my throat. Jill was staring at me with a hurt-puppy look that made me wish very much to strangle her; instead I stepped around the bed, to the window, flung it open. Mist poured in like smoke, and I felt the clouds gather above. "Don't go driving anywhere," I told Jill. "Winter storm warning," and I passed out through the window, into the fog and the swirling snow of the storm.

I remember little between the beginning of the storm and my arrival in this room, but my brain is full of images of swirling snow, and of lightning dancing back and forth between clouds, and throwing my rage down on the helpless Earth below me.

The storm cleared as suddenly as it had arrived, leaving me numb, as I sit here before this infernal machine. Now I am no longer cold, but I think I am still numb, and able to wonder, in a distant, abstract sort of way, what sensation will come to fill the void once the numbness has worn off.

I'm feeling about the same as before, although perhaps it isn't quite as intense. After typing up what happened, I sat very still for a while, then went down to Jim. He said hello, and looked at me for just a moment. He asked me what had happened, and I just shook my head. He waited for a few minutes, and when I still didn't say anything he took himself upstairs. I realized that he was reading what I'd just written, and that made me uncomfortable at first, but there were so many conflicting passions clamoring for my attention that I finally realized I didn't care, so I just waited, wondering what he'd say.

When he came back down he asked me to explain it to him. I was not entirely certain that I could, and told him so. He said, "But this can't be the first time something like this has happened."

"Something like what?" I said.

He frowned, and I got the impression that talking of such things made him uncomfortable, which, just then, was fine by me; I was still in the grip of some nameless combination of emotions in which anger was, if not dominant, at least a part; I badly wanted to strike out at something or someone. In any case, he said, "Discovering that your lover has someone else."

" 'Lover,' " I said. "Now there's an interesting word for it."

He continued to stare past my shoulder, at my chest, or occasionally at my forehead. "What word would you prefer?"

"How about 'victim.' "

"Susan is your victim?"

"No," I said, the word out before I actually thought about it.

"Well, then?"

"If she's a lover, than she's the first lover I've had since . . ."

"Yes?"

"Since Laura."

"Kellem?"

"That's right."

"So this *hasn't* happened before."

"No. Other times, like with Jill, if there's someone in her life, I either ignore him or deal with him, as the case may be."

"But this is different."

"That's right," I said. "This is different."

"What are you going to do about it?"

"I don't know."

"Are you going to kill her?"

"Susan?"

"No, this friend of hers."

"Oh. Jennifer. No, I'm not going to kill her. I wouldn't do that to Susan."

"Yo shonuff gots it, don'cha?"

"Cut it out."

Jim graced me with one of his rare smiles and said nothing else.

After several minutes I said, "So, what would you do?"

"What would *I* do? Why ask me? I'm not even alive."

"You're more alive than most of the people I pass on the street. Besides, what does being alive have to do with anything? You're human, aren't you? What would you do?"

He turned around and watched the cold fireplace for a moment, then he said, "I don't know, Jack."

"Thanks a lot," I said.

He just shrugged. I heard myself growling, and I suddenly wanted to take myself away from there. It was exactly the same as when I'd run away from Jill so I wouldn't kill her, although I knew I couldn't really hurt Jim.

I take that back. I think I *could* hurt Jim, and perhaps I even have. But leave that; there is no way I can hurt Jim *physically.* I thought I ought to type until the feeling passed, but it hasn't.

I must get out of the house for a while.

I'm back once more, feeling maybe just a little better, and a little worse at the same time. I left the house and walked about in the immediate neighborhood, until at last all the walls came down, and then I ran. I jumped the fence into Bill's yard, and there was a growl and a yelp and whine, and then I was gone.

Sometime later I remember walking the streets. I can't tell you how warm or cold it was, or whether there was a wind, or what people or animals were on the street. I just walked.

I eventually made my way to Little Philly, and found where the girls were enduring the cold. I picked a tall black girl named Stacy who had long legs and a haughty look that set my teeth on edge.

She said, "Hey, honey, wanna date?"

I said, "Sure, honey. I don't have a car. Where do you live?"

"Not far, sweets."

"I have the money," I said. "You have the product."

She laughed a phony laugh and showed me to a greasy-looking hotel, and when I left she was no longer wearing her haughty look. I left her with a hundred dollars, which was five times what she'd asked, and I left her still healthy enough that she'd probably survive, which I had not originally intended. I didn't care a great deal if she didn't; I'm perfectly willing to let the embalmers finish what I start.

I came back home after that, and I sit here filled with that horrible mixture of physical well-being and emotional self-disgust that I've had before on such occasions, which is, at any rate, a distraction from thoughts of Susan.

It makes no sense to me that I should feel this way about picking up whores, though; if it is still the remainder of my upbringing (my parents belonged to the Reformation Church and took it very seriously), then all I can say is that one's upbringing has more power than even the head doctors think, because I don't know one of them who has ever said that childhood conditioning can stay with you beyond the grave.

NINE

urge *v.* —*tr.* 1. To drive forward or onward forcefully;
impel; spur . . . *n.* . . . 2. An irresistible or impelling
force, influence, or instinct.

AMERICAN HERITAGE DICTIONARY

Another day passed. Physically, I'm as well as I have ever
been; I feel young and full of energy. Some of this has
crept into my mood, I suppose because the mind wants
to follow the body wherever it may lead. But I am now
feeling more rational about Susan and Jennifer.

No, I certainly am not going to kill Jennifer, nor am
I going to harm Susan in any way; although we certainly
must find an opportunity to talk. But that need not be
today. I do not wish to see Jill again until she has had a
chance to make a more complete recovery, and as for
Susan, well, she obviously did not think she was doing
anything wrong, and perhaps, by her lights, she wasn't.
And in a sense I have invaded her life; it seems that it
behooves me to, if not follow her rules, at least to pay
some attention to them.

For today, at least, I cast all of this aside. I turn my
attention to my dear old friend Laura Kellem; for if,
within my limitations, I can thwart her, I will do so. I

must recognize the truth that Susan has another lover; she is no less herself, and my life remains sweeter for her share in it. I will live if I can.

The last reddish tint of sunset is fading, and my typing room is warmer than usual, I suppose because the sun, weak though she be, has visited my sanctum and prepared it for me.

Some days ago, I think the day after Susan told me about her lover, I was walking through Little Philly and I chanced to overhear a lady, speaking to her companion, give forth a piece of contemporary folk wisdom: "The world would be easier to live in if men weren't stupid and women weren't crazy."

At the time I noted it but gave it no thought. Now it comes back to me, and I think that, if it is not altogether wrong (no folk wisdom is altogether wrong; that's its nature), then at least it is wrong with respect to me. It refers, I think, to how slow men are to see what is before them, and how given women are to self-deception and wild variations of mood. If so, then I am more woman than man, if I am not, in fact, androgynous in this fashion.

I say this because I am discovering how much variation of mood commands my activity. At first, reflecting on Susan's infidelity, I had been shocked, and so had done things of which I was not proud; pride—true, honest pride—is always the result of overcoming our animal nature, of acting in accordance with principles or ideals which have been learned, cognized, and assimilated.

The athlete who takes pride in running faster than another knows that he has overcome his natural lethargy and trained his body to accept the punishment of the race. The musician who takes pride in his composition or his performance has the right to be proud, because he has created an expression of his discipline and his control.

Insofar as we may do a good thing from instinct, we feel, or ought to feel, less pride in the accomplishment than if we had done it through self-control and careful thought; through the domination of the brain over the body. I think my entire life is an effort to secure the command of my brain over my body.

I was not proud, then, that in my frustration I allowed my animal nature to guide me, and as I sat in this room a few scant hours ago and felt sleep overtaking me, I believed that I had come to terms with this nature, and could face Susan's actions as a rational man. But, as I slept, the animal returned, for as I dreamed my mind created images of Susan and Jennifer; what they might be doing together, the things that perhaps they would say—difficult, because I do not know Jennifer's appearance, nor do I ever wish to. In the end, I lay awake, unable to move, unable to control my thoughts. Would I care as much if her lover were a man? Would I care more? I cannot tell; all of the tremblings of rage, of fear, of hurt, and of confusion cry out for some sort of action; experience tells me that anything I do from such a motive will diminish me in my own eyes. It seemed to be hours that I lay there alone with these thoughts, gnashing my teeth and cursing under my breath.

When at last I was able to rise, I came back to my typewriting sanctuary, to set down these thoughts, hoping the expression would be the cure. There is no question that it is moods that guide me, much more than thought, and I am not happy in this realization.

Today, therefore, I shall avoid Susan, and I shall likewise avoid doing anything that I am driven to do by any impetus save cold, logical thought. I will remain in this room for hours if necessary, typing if I feel the need, pacing if that seems helpful. I will conquer this demon ere the night falls.

The brash coals of reason
Linger long once passion's edge
Has curled the kindling paper black and
    brown;
And elected, for a season,
To stammer, halt, and hedge;
The smoke billows, ashes blow around
And inspect each nook before they kiss the
    ground.

I can't believe the coals will burn,
I can't believe they'll die,
I long to track the rising, fading gray
Remains that twist and turn
And melt into the sky;
If heart and mind were one I'd surely stay;
If the coals were out I'd surely go away.

I slept well and without dreams, except that I knew,
somehow, that Jill was feeling better. I resolved to pay
her a visit to celebrate her recovery, as it were, and I
further determined that I would neither avoid Susan nor
seek her out; my feelings toward her remain ambivalent
but not hostile.

It was in this mood, then, that I arrived at Jill's
home. I debated for some few moments whether to
knock, with the attendant risk of meeting Susan, or simply to enter, but in the end I struck the knocker, and to
my surprise, it was Jill who let me in; Jill who was now
dressed, and seemed largely restored to health; Jill who,
upon seeing me, stared at me with wide eyes, and opened
the door with trembling hand; Jill who, after I had entered, closed the door behind me and stood looking at
me, as if waiting for a signal.

I felt the warmth of hunger fall on me like the first
stirrings of love, and I motioned her to me; she came

obediently enough. I tried to be careful with her, so as not to cause a relapse. I brought her up to her bed and laid her down carefully. Her eyes, which had been closed, fluttered open. It was only then that I remembered that I had some questions I had wanted to ask her. She appeared healthy, except that her breathing was the slightest bit rapid and maybe deeper than usual.

"Jill," I said softly.

She looked at me and waited, placidly.

"A few days ago, you and Young Don conspired against me." Tears sprang up in her eyes, I suppose at the mention of Don; I felt a flare of temper, and, at the same time, noticed from the widening of her eyes that she seemed suddenly afraid; I suppose thinking that I intended further revenge upon her. I said, "Do you remember?"

She barely nodded.

I said, "Did Don tell you what to do to your room?"

She nodded again.

"How did he learn?"

She frowned at me, as if she didn't understand the question. I said, "Did he say anything, anything at all, that could tell me how he found out what to do?"

She struggled for a moment, then said in a whisper, "He said he . . ." and her voice trailed off. For a moment I thought she had fainted, for her eyes rolled in her head and then closed, but when I shook her slightly they opened again.

I repeated the question. She said, "He said he had found someone who understood these things."

"Didn't you ask him who?"

She nodded.

"Well?" I said.

"He said it was a woman."

For some reason, my thoughts jumped instantly to

Kellem, although that didn't make sense. I said, "Did he give you her name?"

She shook her head.

"Didn't he say anything about her at all?"

"No," she said. "I asked, but all he said was that she was sickening."

"Sickening?"

She nodded.

"That was the word he used?"

She nodded again.

I frowned. An odd way to describe someone who—

Oh. I laughed then, because it was funny. *Sickening.* Yes, indeed.

I left her sleeping peacefully. Then, in spite of my good intentions, I knocked on Susan's door, but there was no answer, and I heard no one breathing within, so I returned home. I am filled with a sort of nervous energy and wish I knew whither to direct it. I want to find Susan and talk to her; I want to do something about Kellem, I want to pursue these hints I received from Jill. Instead, I sit here and I type.

But, all right, so there is some "sickening" person (that really is a delightful joke) who knows a few things that are better forgotten; that doesn't mean she's out there, staying up nights thinking of ways to get me. There are too many stories of men running headlong into their fate in an effort to avoid it. I will disregard her for now, and merely note her existence for later use.

Note: don't forget sickening woman.

There. It's noted.

And now, by all the angels of the pit, I've had enough of this. I am going back there, and if Susan isn't in, I will wait; and then I don't know. I think, in any case, that I can be certain I won't do anything that

* * *

As I look at the bottom of the last page I typed, I cannot for the life of me think how I meant to end that last sentence. But that was yesterday, and a great deal has happened since then. None of it really important, I suppose, but interesting nevertheless. I was typing away gayly, speculating on going to visit Susan, when I heard the sounds of the door being forced. At almost the same time, Jim appeared in front of me.

"Jack," he said.

"Yes, the door." I was already rising and looking for a place to hide the sheaf of papers. "Is it the police?"

"I don't think so," he said. "They didn't bother knocking."

"They might think we're armed and dangerous."

"They might."

I decided it would take too long to hide the papers, so I had to be contented with hiding myself and them along with me, which I did by entering the closet of my sanctuary and pulling myself up through the little rectangular door in the ceiling and so up into the attic. I hoped I wouldn't have to stay there long; it was even colder than the room, there being no insulation to speak of; hadn't Professor Carpenter ever heard of energy conservation?

There were still those boxes of books, and I found Geoffrey of Monmouth's *History of the Kings of Britain* and amused myself with it for a while. After a wait of perhaps twenty minutes, Jim came up to the attic, passing through the trap door and sitting next to me on one of the horizontal struts that were the only floor the attic had.

"I wonder why they never finished this," I said. "It could be a good, usable area."

"Never needed it, I guess. The people who built it only had one child, and the people they sold it to only had two. Professor Carpenter never had any."

"Yeah. So, who are our guests?"

"Well, they surely aren't the police."

"Do tell."

"There's two of them, both in their thirties, both pretty dirty-looking."

"They come here to rob the place?"

"No, I think they just want a place to stay."

I swore; Jim winced.

I said, "What are they doing?"

"Just sitting, talking quietly."

"What about?"

"The house, the neighborhood, how likely they are to be disturbed."

"So they know no one lives here?"

"Apparently. One of them said that his little brother had just spent the night here." Jim's expression was wry.

I smirked. "I told you we should have—"

"No doubt," said Jim.

I shrugged. "What do they have with them?"

"They each have a suitcase."

"Big?"

"Small."

"Should we try to stay out of their way, or drive them from us?"

"Why ask me?" said Jim. "I'm not risking anything, and, as far as I'm concerned, the more the better. I like the company."

I scowled at him, then slipped down from the attic, careful not to make any noise. I made my way to the top of the stairs and looked and listened. There was very little light, and what there was glowed an unusual white. I smelled the harsh, familiar odor of a camp lantern, and, after listening carefully, heard the characteristic hiss it gave out. Our visitors weren't saying much just at this time, but I heard the dull, hollow clank metal gives off when it strikes glass, and the sounds of tools being manipulated. This aroused my curiosity, so I ventured down the stairs a little, and very carefully poked my head out.

There wasn't much light at all; I could see two men, both rather large. One was bearded, and the other one had a face that reminded me of the French countryside after the Great War. Both were very pale in the white glow of the lantern. They were sitting on the floor, working with something I couldn't make out. The suitcases were open, however, and I could see the contents, which answered all mysteries.

I had to clench my teeth and cover my mouth to keep from laughing; it took me a minute or two to get it under control. Then I considered whether to consult Jim or to simply resolve the situation. I decided that Jim had left it up to me, so I vaulted over the railing from the landing to the floor, letting my shoes slap the ground. I think the effect was augmented by the black clothing I happened to be wearing, so they probably couldn't see me very well.

One of them out-and-out screamed, the other gave an inarticulate cry, dropped what he was working on, and reached into the pocket of his jacket. I waited until he had the gun out so he'd feel better, and a few seconds later the other one was also holding a weapon of some sort, both weapons being pointed generally in my direction.

"Good evening," I said pleasantly. "May I help you gentlemen with something?"

The one with the beard said, "Who the f—— are you?"

"I live here," I said. "And you?"

They looked at each other, and the bearded one stood. I could see that he was holding some sort of very large pistol; perhaps a machine pistol, although I had never seen one up close.

"You don't live here," said the beard, flatly. I waited

for the other one to say "That's right, if Lefty says you don't live here, then you don't," but he didn't say anything. I think he hadn't gotten over his fright.

I said, "I beg to differ. And I'm afraid I must ask you to leave. You may take your possessions with you."

I had the impression that they were both terrified, and terrified people are unpredictable. I have found that, ironically, fear often drives people into making the worst possible decision.

"F——," said the beard, and made the worst possible decision. Yes, it was indeed a machine pistol, and I was not at all happy with what it did to the woodwork. Pock-face fired too, a second later, and, though he didn't have an automatic weapon, it was a very large bullet, and made a real mess of the wainscoting.

When they had stopped their noise-making, they just stared at me. After a moment, Pock-face said, very softly, "Jesus Christ."

Jim came down a moment later, and when he saw what had been done to the woodwork, I swear he almost cried. I said, "Do you think someone may have heard the shooting?"

"Huh?" he said. "Maybe."

"Then I should clean up—" which was as far as I got before I saw flashing lights through one of the uncovered and unbroken windows on the main floor. I took the pistol because it came to mind that I might need one, dashed upstairs once more, and hid the pistol in the attic. I was trying to figure out what to do when I heard the door open, and a voice called out, "Police!" This was repeated several times.

Jim was next to me. "They have a dog," he said.

"I know; I smell it."

"What are you going to do?"

"What worries me," I said, "is that, if they think

there's someone here, they'll keep looking until they find someone."

"But then—"

"On the other hand," I said, "they do have a dog."

I made my way silently to another bedroom, one with an unbroken window. I opened it, and the cold air rushed in. They were being very cautious downstairs; they had found the bodies, and must assume someone else was in the house; they had probably seen two sets of footprints entering through the snow, and none leaving.

I saw the beam of a flashlight from outside just in time to duck back from the window. The easy part was getting out the window, down to an imperfectly sealed and very small basement window, into the basement, and into my hideyhole, all without being seen. The hard part was convincing the dog that I had gone directly up the stairs, into the bedroom, and out the window. From there, I *could* have gone onto the roof and down a tree, landing on the dry pavement of the alley behind the house.

It must have worked, because they didn't make an exhaustive search of the house, although I could hear them for hours, going over every inch of the living room. They must have been efficient, however, because by the next evening they were gone, taking the bodies and other evidence with them. The doors have been sealed with yellow tape that reads, "Crime Site, Sealed by Order of the Police Department," and a placard citing the ordinance that gives them permission to do this, and threatens imprisonment of up to five years, fines of up to one hundred thousand dollars, or both to anyone breaking the seal or disturbing the scene. I am not terribly worried.

When I looked at the mess on the main floor, the first thing I noticed was that they had removed large sections of the woodwork, apparently taking every piece in which a bullet was embedded, which annoyed me and

made poor Jim miserable. I don't think he was happy
about the stains on the polished maple floor, either, but
what choice did I have?

After commiserating with him for a few minutes, I
came up to the typewriting room, found the typewriting
machine undisturbed and the papers still in the attic, and
set to work recording what had happened, which brings
me, Constant Reader, up to the very minute.

I have been sitting here thinking and remembering my
thoughts as I lay waiting for the police to either find me
or not. I don't know if these thoughts are sufficiently
organized to set down, but let me try.

It seems that attitudes toward criminals have
changed substantially since I was a child. It may be that
I am wrong, because I was largely sheltered from contact
with those sorts of people until I met Laura, but it seems
that, when I was young, one was a criminal, or one was
an honest citizen, and the demarcation was well drawn.
Today, most people break laws and don't think much of
it, perhaps because of the odd things that have come to
be illegal. But the result is that the line between law-
abiding citizen and hardened criminal is much softer
than it was.

It seems clear to me that our visitors of last night
were criminals in every sense of the word, but one of
them had a little brother who acted the way any young
man might have. So, did something go "wrong" with his
older brother? Or does being a criminal mean something
different than it did years ago? Jill is a criminal too,
because there were marijuana buds in her ashtray, but is
she like the gentlemen from last night? Or like the three
children who were here before? When I was much
younger, and far more naïve, I thought that the line
between legal and illegal stayed close to the line between
right and wrong. Well, either I was living an illusory life

then, or everything has changed now, so that when the two lines intersect it seems only momentary, transitory, coincidental.

Or, more likely, it is because when I do what I must to survive, I am, technically, committing crimes; yet how can what I do be wrong, when it is only what I must do? Still, perhaps this is a justification that has been used by scoundrels ever since the class has existed; I do not know.

I wish I could listen to some music. I'm hearing Chopin in my head, and I would love to truly hear it. With the police nosing around the house, though, I wouldn't dare put in a stereo system even if I had one.

Hell, I'm a criminal; I could steal one; I've been stealing electricity all along. I suppose Professor Carpenter pays the dollar or two a month to keep it on and hasn't noticed the six or seven cents it costs to run the water pump. I'm glad the place has its own well so that after I managed to turn the water on I didn't have to worry about him suddenly getting unexplained bills from the city.

I wish, for Jim's sake, that the woodwork hadn't gotten messed up.

I have just returned from Susan's. It occurs to me that I never saw Jill, nor even asked about her. It was a mad and crazy time, and in the end, I nearly—well, it doesn't matter, I didn't. When I think of how close I came it does give me to tremble.

I have never been one to rail against the gods, but that passion should be so dangerous is a crime. I do not know what I have done that I should be punished in this way; that the more I love, the more I must fight myself, or else the more I will kill. I know, I *know* that someday I will lose control, and take her life, and on that day I will weep.

But let me set it down as well as I can remember

it—and this, I think, I will be able to set down verbatim, because it is branded on all the cells that constitute my brain. In fact, it may not be necessary to record it, for I cannot imagine a time when the memory will grow dim.

But I will set it down anyway, because in that way I can live it again.

The two roommates from upstairs—I forget their names—were just leaving as I arrived. They nodded to me vaguely, as if they couldn't remember who I was but thought we might have met once. I knocked on the door, and this time it was Susan who answered. She greeted me with a big smile and showed me in.

"Hello," I said. "And how are we today?"

"Perky and chipper," she sang, and twirled around the room, ending in a classic ballet pose, one arm over her head, the other in front of her, knees bent, one foot pointed down, head tilted and face in a china-doll smile.

I bowed gracefully and held out my hand. She took it, I bowed, she curtsied, and we waltzed around the room, *sans* music, for a minute or two, before I twirled her away. She finally stopped in the same pose that had started the dance, held it for a moment, dimpled, then bowed. I said, "Let's chat."

"Hmmm?" she said. "Something on your mind?"

"How many lovers do you have, my dear?"

Her face clouded for a moment, but it was only a cirrus, no thunderhead in sight, and presently it went away, leaving a few pale wisps of puzzled expression in its wake. She said, "Don't you think that a rather personal question, Jonathan?"

"Well, yes, but I'm a daring individual that way. How many lovers *do* you have?"

She stood straight, her arms folded, and she frowned an enchanting frown while she decided whether to answer me. At last she said, "You and Jennifer. Why? Do you think I need more?"

I laughed in spite of myself. "Why? Because I am mad with jealousy, my dear. Simply mad. Can't you tell?"

"*Are* you jealous, Jonathan?"

I sighed. "I'm not entirely certain. If so, it's the first time. No, the second, actually. But the first was a long time ago, and about someone it wasn't worth being jealous about. You are."

"Tell me about it."

"Guess."

"Your friend—what was her name?"

"Laura."

"You were jealous of her?"

"I think so. Actually, I think there was a time when she wanted me to be jealous, and I tried to oblige but I didn't quite manage."

"Why?"

"It was toward the end of our romance, and I think she wanted to end it with me leaving her instead of having to break it off."

"She didn't want to hurt you."

"Maybe. Or she didn't want to be annoyed. She was quite capable of taking the long way around if it would save her some annoyance."

Susan looked sad. "I like to play games, Jonathan. But I don't want you to ever think I'm playing games with your feelings. I'll never do that, and I'll be very sad if you ever think I am."

"I don't think you are, Susan."

"Good. Then what are we going to do?"

"I don't know. I don't know if we have to *do* anything."

"I don't want you to be unhappy."

"My happiness isn't your responsibility."

"I know that. But still—"

"Yes. I understand."

"What did it feel like, when you were jealous?"

"It was ugly, but only slightly ugly."

"What does this feel like?"

"It's uglier."

She walked up to me (actually, it was more like *cross c to r*) and put her hands on my shoulders. She looked directly into my eyes and said, "You don't expect me to leave Jennifer, do you?"

I kept very careful control over myself and said, "No. I don't expect you to, and I'm not asking you to."

She remained where she was and said, "Well, then?"

"I don't know." I felt myself smile a little. "You are giving me a new experience, for which I thank you."

"You're welcome," she said, and kissed my mouth lightly.

"However," I said, "I'm not exactly certain what to do, or, for that matter, what I feel."

"I know what I feel," said Susan. "I love you."

I was hit by a sudden, and mercifully brief, sense of vertigo. The heavens were uprooted and the world spun around me, and all I could think was, *This is real. I did not make her do this, this is real. This is real.*

Now that I think about it, the only other time in my life I've felt anything like that is when Young Don got me with the shotgun; there was the same onrush of significance in waves, and the same disorientation, and feeling of, *Has my life been nothing but a preparation for this moment?* I let the waves pass over me, not really caring if I drowned in them.

When I had regained my equilibrium and opened my eyes again, I found that she was still staring directly into them. I put my hands very lightly on her waist. "That," I said, "is not one of the possibilities."

Her eyes widened. "How not?" she said.

"It just isn't."

She took my hand and began leading me up the stairs. "I think I can prove you're wrong," she said.

"Yes," I said. "You probably can."

And she did, too.

TEN

AMERICAN HERITAGE DICTIONARY

An unsatisfying sort of day. I was feeling lazy at first, so
I just sat around talking to Jim for a while. I asked him
if he had ever married. He said, "Oh, yes. Had three
children, too. The youngest was born a free man."

"What ever became of them?"

"They moved away. They're all dead now. We never
saw much of them, except for the one who . . ." His voice
trailed off and he looked troubled.

"Who what?" I said.

"Who was . . . different."

"Retarded?"

"No."

"Crippled?"

"It doesn't matter. We kept her with us, and it was
all right. But she couldn't have gotten an education anyway, because she was a girl as well as a Negro, so it
doesn't matter. She was a sweet little girl, all her life."

I looked at him for a while, wanting to ask him more

about his family, but then I decided that perhaps I should not. He said, "You ever married?"

"I was engaged once."

"Oh? What happened?"

"I met Kellem."

"Oh. I wonder if she was ever married."

"Yes, she was."

"Really? What ever became of her husband?"

"Make a guess, Jim."

He frowned. "You mean, she—"

"Right."

"Oh." He spent some time thinking about that, then looked at my chest again and said, "I wonder if that bothers her."

I threw away a snappy answer and actually thought about it, wondering too, but I couldn't make up my mind. How much of Laura did it explain? What happens when you're driven to something by your animal needs and then come to regret it? I don't know. I avoid that problem by never doing anything I'll have cause to regret, but in her case—

Rubbish. What difference does it make? She is who she is, and how she got that way is none of my concern.

Still, it does give one to think.

Jim said, "You've been writing a great deal."

"Yes," I said. "It eases my mind."

He frowned. "Sometimes when you say things, I don't know if you're being ironic."

"Sometimes neither do I," I said.

"Well?"

"Well what?"

"Why *are* you so involved in writing down everything that happens?"

I shrugged. It made me uncomfortable to talk about; I don't know why. I said, "When it's all done I'll have it published and I'll become a famous author."

"Now," he said, "you are being ironic."

"Yes."

"I had a friend who wrote a book once."

"Oh?"

"He said it was more work than it was worth."

"It probably is," I said.

We drifted off onto other subjects that I don't remember very well. After a while I became restless and left, making my way over to Susan's, where I made certain that she was alone before I knocked on the door.

She was in a mood to go out, so I took her to a motion picture at one of those places with about nineteen screens under one roof. The picture was called *Another 48 Hours,* and it was an enjoyable film, if mindless. I thought the girl in the cage was quite attractive.

So did Susan.

After the movie we went back to her house and sat around for a while, just talking.

She said, "Jonathan, are you ever going to spend the night with me?"

I felt, I admit, a certain thrill at the question, along with worry that she might insist on an answer. I said, "I'm glad that you want me to."

We were sitting on the couch, my arm about her shoulders. She moved a little closer to me. I said, "There will be a time to talk of the future, perhaps, but now isn't it."

"I hadn't been speaking about the rest of our lives."

"No. Nor am I encouraging you to. If we decide that we want to talk of such things, we always can. There is no need to just now, don't you think?"

"I agree," she said, which took care of the discussion of sleeping arrangements for the moment. I moved toward her, pressing her very gently back onto the couch. I was careful; she was so very, very sweet.

Sometime later I returned home to this faithful typewriting machine to pour out my confusions; or, at any rate, to recount the experiences of the day. Now they are recounted, and there is nothing to add.

I went over to the Tunnel today to look at the sights and to think. There was a tall, bearded, scraggly-looking fellow standing in the recess of a building, and as I passed he asked if I could give him some money.

"No," I said.

He said, "Are you sure, man? Even five dollars would help."

That stopped me. I turned to him and said, "Five dollars? *Five* dollars? What happened to 'can you spare a dime'?"

He looked puzzled, and I walked on. If I'd been him, I'd have made a remark about inflation, but I don't think he was of entirely sound mind. The result, however, was that I happened to notice a United Way billboard that I'd passed a hundred times before, and it got me thinking about charities.

I've never given anything to charity; I don't know why. I am not a heartless man, but something about giving money to I know not what organization to do I know not what with is repugnant to me. I have helped my friends when they needed help, and I expect them to do the same, and it isn't even that I don't care what happens to complete strangers, and don't wish them the best.

Maybe it's that it all seems so futile.

No answers, here, but it is another thing to think about, since I seem to have become involved in self-examination lately, for whatever reason.

Everyone, and I include myself, has a need, I think, to feel that he is helping other people. Some of us limit it to friends, others want to help strangers, while still others eschew what they consider trivialities and find whatever cause seems to them to strike at either the most important issues or the most fundamental. It's hard to say that any of these methods is better or worse than any others.

No, I take that back. I don't like being approached on the street, or by charities, because they make me think that I owe something because I have a share in whatever brought them to this state, and that is untrue and irritating. Whether it is some bum standing on the street, or a huge billboard depicting starving children in Africa, they are saying, "If your life is better than this, it's your fault mine isn't as good," and I just won't accept the guilt for that. I didn't build this world, I don't control it, and when I succor a friend, or even a stranger, it is because I want to.

I feel no shame because, though I bear the guilt for my actions, I refuse to accept blame for things with which I had nothing to do, and I don't do things for which I ought to feel shame.

I am not without a conscience; I merely have no need for shame.

10 March
Traci Kaufmann
2216 N. 7th St.
Apt 11A
Akron, OH
Dear Traci:

I hope this letter finds you well. It is some time since we have corresponded, and, if I may, correspondingly longer since we have seen each other in the flesh, but memories, as they say, linger on, and we have more than our share of those.

Had I received a letter from you like this, my first thought should have been, "What does she want of me?" I do not doubt that this same thought, with regard to myself, is flashing across your brain. Well, I will pretend to nothing different. A situation has come up in which you could help me immeasurably. Are you traveling these days? Is there an airport in Akron? I can certainly send you money for tickets.

As to the service itself, well, I have no doubt that you can guess its nature, but let the details wait until we are together again. Should you be uninterested in helping me, well, come anyway, and we can sit around and remember evenings in Belgrade, and nights in Vienna.

I am including my address. Please let me know if you are free, and, if so, when.

I Remain, as Always,
Your Servant,
Jack Agyar

I met Bill once more today. It was still early evening, and he was out prowling the neighborhood with a determined look on his face. I stopped and said hello. He said, "Have you seen any stray dogs around here?"

"No," I said. "Can't say I have. Did Pepper run off?"

He shook his head. "No. Another dog got into our yard and killed her."

"Oh. I'm sorry. What did it look like?"

"I don't know; I didn't see it. It must have been big, though, judging from what it did to Pepper."

I winced and repeated that I was sorry.

"Well," he said. "I'm going to be keeping a close eye out around here, and I've been asking everyone else to do the same."

"I will."

"Good."

He nodded and went on his way, looking pathetically determined.

I got to Susan's house, and, once more, checked to see if she was alone. This time I heard soft voices in the bedroom, and I assumed one of them was Jennifer's.

For just a second I wanted to break the window and descend on them in a storm of blood and anger, then I thought to escape entirely; to go far away where I'd be out of the reach of such thoughts. My next idea was to enter and pay Jill a visit, but I did not trust myself sufficiently; it would be inconvenient if she were to die.

In the end, I sat there, a cold wind blowing across my body, and I studied the stars through the passing wisps of clouds, undimmed by any moon. I do not know how long I waited there, or what I thought I was waiting for, but I suddenly became aware that the door had opened, and Jennifer had left the house.

I remember thinking that her step was very distinct; she leaned forward a bit as she walked, so the scuffling sound came after the step, almost as if she were skating. To my eyes, as I followed her, she was a dark blur against a dark street, but I could follow the pinpoints of the occasional porch or living-room light that she blotted out as she passed before them.

It would have been so easy to fall on her then, as she walked, and have done with it, and I do not know why I didn't do so. But in the end she came to a very small house, all dark inside with a heavily textured roof and a squat chimney to which a TV antenna was attached. The house did not seem to have many windows. As I watched, a half-moon rose and made the stars fade just a little.

I thought, then, about knocking on the door and seeing if she wanted to invite me in for a chat, but it didn't seem to be such a good idea because I wasn't certain what to say to her, or how I'd feel if she did, in fact, did not wish to talk to me. I had to assume she knew about me; did it bother her? Did I care if it did?

If it means so much, why am I so confused and ashamed at my own feelings? If it means so little, why do I feel betrayed whenever I know they are together?

I've written a letter to an old friend who could solve this problem for me, but now I'm not certain if I want to send it. I guess I'll just leave it sitting here for a while and decide later.

Exhaustion, weakness, and trembling are, I think, a small price to pay for life and freedom. We can call that tonight's lesson and be done with it, but where's the fun in that? This evening I have had a brush with death or captivity, and learned something important. At this moment, the effects of the escape are so strong that I cannot determine what I have learned, but the exhaustion, I know, will pass.

I remember that, when I rose, the thought was with me that I had not seen Jill for some days, and it wouldn't do for the poor dear to feel neglected, so, after showering and brushing my teeth, I put on my coat and went out to find her. I could just as easily have brought her to me, but it was a clear, if cold, night, with the stars showing as much of themselves as they dared to in the city; the Big Dipper wheeled over my head and Orion smiled down on me.

Or so I thought at the time. Now, I wonder if he was not laughing at me; but that is as much nonsense as the other; the stars are merely stars, and I put no more weight on their attitudes than I do on dreams.

Numerology, on the other hand, is a proven fact.

That was a joke, Jim.

To continue, then, it was still early in the evening, well before moonrise, and Fullerton was still busy with rush-hour traffic. I was just turning onto Twenty-sixth when I felt a light hit my face—one of those lights that you instantly realize has been directed at you.

The heart is like the stomach—one doesn't notice its existence until it misbehaves. Now in my case—but never mind. I stopped, turned, and looked directly into the light, which was painful, but I didn't know what else to do. I waited, feeling as if all of my nerve endings were on top of my skin.

I heard two car doors open at once, and the unmistakable voice of officialdom said, "Hey, buddy, can I talk to you for a minute?" I had to decide what to do right then; there was no time for thought. Had I considered it, I might have allowed them to arrest me, because there were things to learn at the police station. But as I said, there was no time. I could, I think, have killed them, but I have been given to understand that killing policemen is not something to be undertaken lightly; so I turned and ran.

One of them yelled "Stop, asshole!" which gave rise to some scatological thoughts that would have been funny under other circumstances. I tried to think as I ran. There are things I can do that could keep me hidden, but they take time. I could certainly outrun them to get the time, but I can't outrun bullets.

I found an alley, ducked into it, and saw that it did not dead-end. This wasn't entirely luck; I have noticed that Lakota tends toward alleys that run from street to street. I heard their footsteps behind me, and one of them was threatening to shoot. Did he mean it? What did they want me for? Under what circumstances, if any, were they allowed to shoot fleeing suspects? I suspected they would stay within their rules (I was, after all, white, and at the worst wanted for a simple, if violent, crime), but I didn't know what those rules were.

I took a gamble and just ran. I heard one of them cursing, very faintly. They were a good distance behind me; perhaps fifty yards. What would they do now? Call for assistance? Did they have hand units, or would they need to return to their car?

Fifty yards ought to take a man in good condition but weighed down with gun, nightstick, etc., at least five seconds to run. More like ten or even fifteen, but call it five. Enough? Maybe.

I tried to order my mind while running, and after a few steps realized that all I was accomplishing was to run more slowly and lose some of the lead I had built up.

I turned a corner, took five steps, and stopped. I was on a residential street running parallel to and a block from the Ave. It was a busy street: three lanes of one-way traffic, but no businesses were at hand to lend too much light to the proceedings. The nearest street lamp bathed me in its cone of luminance. It's funny, the sort of details one notices.

Some factors that I considered: The weather in Lakota comes off Lake Erie, and is unpredictable at the best of times, winter not being the best of times. There were mounds of dirty, plowed snow built up off the sidewalk and spilling over onto the street. Furthermore, it was a rather humid day for midwinter.

I heard footfalls, and started off again, at a good pace, but only walking. There was a weakness in my legs that I liked not at all. I heard mutterings behind me, as if one of my pursuers were speaking, followed by a hum of white noise; yes, they could call for help without returning to their car. They were doing so.

It occurred to me, then, that the car was unattended.

There were curses behind me, and "Where the Hell did *this* come from?"

Was it worth taking the chance?

I kept walking, hurrying as much as I could but remaining silent; I began to head back the way I'd come. I'd have to move quickly, if at all. A brief moment of dizziness hit me, leaving behind it a sense of weakness in all my limbs; but this was to be expected.

In the midst of a fog (if I may) I came to the car, which was not locked. There were sirens coming toward us and the radio was squawking angrily; someone was reciting numbers with great conviction. I stuck my head into the car and glanced in at the mass of electronic gear, artillery, and Hostess cupcake wrappers.

I was rewarded, if you can call it that, by seeing an unflattering but not too unfaithful sketch of myself, stuck to a clipboard attached to the dashboard. Even as I looked at it, I did not forget what I was about. The fog grew thicker, and seemed to pour into the car; it did not obscure my vision.

The sketch was on a clean, white piece of paper, with today's date written in the upper left corner. There was a number (4-282-6315) hand-lettered in the upper right. Below the sketch were some notes to the effect that I was five eight (I'm actually five six, but I dress to look tall), weigh about a hundred and twenty (more like a hundred and thirty, friend, but thanks), had black hair, black eyes, should be considered armed and dangerous (I'm never armed, but I'm never unarmed either) and that I was a suspect in a homicide investigation at

Damn it to Hell. I just now realized why that address was familiar, which means I know how they must have gotten my description: that fat man who had let me into Young Don's place. But never mind that now.

I read more of what I was supposed to look like until I heard rapidly approaching footsteps on the street behind me.

There is, as many have noted before me, a strength that comes with anger. I felt it then, overcoming my weakness. As the policeman's face became clear in the fog, I had the sudden impression of pale blue eyes and a light-colored mustache, and I know that he had something in his hand, though whether it was a stick, a gun, a radio, or something else entirely I do not know.

But I backed out of the car and faced him faster, I think, than he expected me to; and I know he did not expect me to be on him before he had time to do anything. With one hand I took his arm and with the other his leg. I think I was going to dash him to the street, which would certainly have crushed the life out of him, but in the end I merely threw him as far from me as I could. He gave a cry as he flew, then he hit the ground with a thud and a tinkle of gear, as if I'd thrown a tin soldier.

I stopped and listened carefully. I could hear moaning from the policeman I had thrown, and, even as all of this was happening I was relieved that I had not killed him, but I could hear more sounds—people running, purposefully, in my direction. They were closing in around me.

Even as I noticed that, I saw spotlights attempt to pierce the winter fog. A wild notion came upon me to get into the car and attempt to drive it (were the keys even in it? I never looked, nor did the question cross my mind until now), but my skills with such machines are poor at best, and this would leave me limited, and fighting on their terms.

So I would fight on mine.

I knew they could not yet be completely organized, and they certainly couldn't know what was going on, so, with no hesitation, I charged out at them with all the speed I could manage. I got a glimpse of a couple of confused faces, and I ran into one policeman who had a drawn pistol in his hand and was in the act of leveling it at me; in fact, I leveled him and continued.

There were shouts of "There he goes," and "Call for more backup," but it was, to my ears, more like the bleating of sheep than the baying of hounds. The fog still protected me as I crossed the street and climbed up onto the second story porch of a tall old house; a house that, now that I think of it, is not too dissimilar to Jim's.

I scrabbled up onto the roof (I wonder if anyone in the house heard my footfalls, and, if they did, what they thought was happening) and from there managed, just barely, to reach the roof of the house next to it. I'm glad the houses are close together in that part of the city, and insert same parenthetical remark as above.

There was, by now, a great deal of activity below me; I could make out the flashing lights of several police cars, and I could see where their headlights cut the fog; but they would not look at the rooftops. I took the time to catch my breath, wanting suddenly to laugh aloud at them scurrying around down there like so many ants whose overworked simile has been disturbed.

I didn't laugh, however. After a few moments to recover I made my way home. I was as careful as I could be in my state of anxiety, exhaustion, and weakness; at all events I made it safely into the house without any other incidents.

Jim took one look at me and I think he almost swore. "What happened?" he said.

I closed the window and sank down into the blood-stained gray chair. "The police know what I did—at least some of it—and know what I look like."

He whistled. "Do they know where you live?"

"I don't think so, although, now that you mention it, there are neighbors who know what I look like, and the police are already suspicious of this house, so they might put things together."

"What are you going to do?"

"I don't know. That is, I don't know in the long run."

"What about the short run?"

"For one thing, I'm going to visit Jill first thing tomorrow."

"I would imagine. What else?"

I didn't answer, but I suppose I must have looked disgusted, because Jim said, "What is it?"

"It's how they identified me, curse them. I wouldn't mind all the rest, but . . ."

When I didn't go on, he said, "But what?"

"They know what my coat looks like. I'm going to have to stop wearing it, damn it to Hell."

Predictably, Jim looked disapproving at the profanity, but he also laughed.

"What's so funny?" I said.

"Some guys sure got it rough," he said.

"Go suck astral eggs," I told him, and came up to the typing machine to set it all down.

ELEVEN

a·byss *n.* 1.a. The primeval chaos. b. The bottomless pit; hell. 2. An unfathomable chasm; a yawning gulf. 3. Any immeasurably profound depth or void.

AMERICAN HERITAGE DICTIONARY

A sense of perspective would be helpful now. It is not the end of the world that the police know what I look like. If I can't evade a few cops, I don't deserve to. Can they see in the dark? Can they peer through walls? Hell, I can see them coming well before they see me, if I stay at all alert.

They don't know where I live. They don't where Susan lives. They don't know where I play cards. They don't know the street corners where I pick up hookers; or even that I do so. They know I have a really nice coat, and that means I won't be able to wear it any more. A shame, but I've lived through worse.

Once Laura and I had to hide out in a Paris sewer for three nights and three hellish days; I thought I was going to die. She never told me from whom or what we were hiding. The rats would come and do tricks for us, and moths would fly down and arrange themselves in pretty aerial patterns for us, Laura would tell me stories, and I would make up poems for her, and that was the sum total of our entertainment.

Come to think of it, that was when she told me I ought to be a poet, and after that she made me write every day, which I continued to do until she left me, after which I stopped until just recently.

But that is neither here nor there. What I remember most clearly is that each day I would get weaker, and hungrier; and by the end of the third day, when she decided it was safe again, I couldn't move at all; I just lay there and moaned. She had to carry me out, and she was in scarcely better shape than I was. I remember her warning me on the first day that a knife wound, or even a beating, could be fatal during the hours of daylight, and I thought that it hardly needed any sort of injury at all. She brought us up, somewhere, in an alley, and we lay there together until a drunk stumbled over us, cursing, and that was how we survived.

If I could live through that, I should not be unduly afraid of a couple of police officers who don't even know what they're looking for.

I really do wonder what had happened, though, that sent Kellem and me into hiding in the sewers.

I found a clothing store and I have bought a winter parka. It is hideously ugly, but warm. I'm still annoyed that I can't wear my coat any more, but at least I won't freeze; that is, I won't freeze more than I did going to get the coat. I doubt there will be more than another week or two of winter, but I can afford it, so why not?

As I write this, I am feeling even more worn out and fatigued; exposure will do that.

Why couldn't Kellem have had the courtesy to want to kill me in California? Or, if she was going to insist on Ohio, she could have at least waited until summer.

For that matter, what is it about this city that has so

taken her? It is too small to get lost in, yet too big to relax in. It has neither a climate nor atmosphere such as I would have thought appealed to her. Why not Yellow Springs, if she wanted a coffee-house atmosphere and to live in Ohio? Or, better yet, San Francisco, where she could hop over to Oakland any time she wanted to kill someone; no one cares who dies in Oakland.

I'm feeling angry and frustrated, mostly at Kellem. No, that isn't right; now that I think of it, it is mostly that I am mortally weary.

Well, that is a problem I can solve. A visit with Jill ought to be just the thing. I feel that she is awake, and she awaits me.

I'm back from seeing Jill. It is late and there is a light but chilly breeze coming through the slats covering the window. Jill still seemed pale and listless; I was afraid to tax her strength too much. I feel better for the visit, but not enough, not enough.

I left her sleeping and found Susan, who was in the living room, reading French. For some reason, this set off a chain of fantasies of the two of us in Paris, the way Kellem and I had visited together. But I would never do to Susan what Kellem is doing to me.

Susan remarked that I didn't look well; I said I seemed to have picked up some sort of virus, and she ought not to come too close to me. She blew me a kiss from across the room, and I returned home, watching for the police and taking my time so I wouldn't wear myself out any more than I had to.

I wish I understood more of the process by which these things happen—that is, why some things leave me exhausted, and other things are as easy as falling over. Well, actually, it's not easy to fall over; I have a deeply rooted instinct to catch myself, but the point remains.

There are many things I have learned that I can

do—things that I think Laura ought to have told me about; instead I discover them by accident. This goes for limitations as well. There are times I have found that I could not do something I wanted to; a peculiar feeling, as if my will to take some action were being diverted from outside of myself. Why should this be? And why am I wondering about it now, when I never have before?

But leave all that; it doesn't matter nearly as much as the fact that I am bone-weary and exhausted from all that I did escaping from the police. Seeing Jill helped, but I have not come close to recovering from yesterday's exertions.

I will rest well, and see what tomorrow brings.

Life is a thing of give-and-take, of trading something not so good for something a little better; of exchanging a slight loss for a slight gain.

I am still feeling weak and shaken, but it could have been much, much worse.

Bah.

I cannot deceive myself. I am still enraged. I tell myself that it was a reasonable thing for her to do, and I'd have done the same thing in her position, and it is all true, but it amounts to nothing. I don't know how I resisted destroying her utterly, and, if I continue to feel this way, she will not live to see the snow melt. There are times when I can be rational, and times when I cannot. In this case, she not only betrayed me, but she did so when I was as weak as I've been in a very long time indeed. I require rest, I must recover my strength; I do not need the sort of games she chose, no, *dared* to play with me.

In any case, there is no time to do anything about it tonight.

Shall I describe it in detail? Why? It is not the sort of thing I am likely to forget. On the other hand, why not? It might help settle me down, to concentrate on striking the right key, and on recalling everything as well as possible, and working to get it all in order, even as it happened.

Besides, I am certain that Jim will want to know about it all, and I'd rather he read this than asked me to tell him; if I try to talk I'll probably

Yes. I will set it down.

My intention, then, was to visit Little Philly, and I even did so, resplendent in my ugly new coat. The idea—ha!—was to attempt to spare Jill as much as I could. I spent a few minutes talking to Jim and gathering what strength remained to me, then I walked out the door. I took my time getting to the area, watching carefully for police cars.

Even after arriving there I continued to be careful. I spent several hours observing the scene outside the strip bars and the "adult" bookstores—those ugly, window-less brick buildings looking like prisons to house the trapped desire—until I found what I wanted. She was small and artificially blond, and could not have been more than sixteen years old. She wore a white knee-length coat with imitation fur trim, and slung over her back was a tiny black purse with a long strap. She stood near the curb in front of the door of Lorenzo's Night Club with a cigarette that appeared to be permanently fixed to the corner of her mouth. She was carrying on a conversation with someone in a white Thunderbird, who drove off as I watched. I came up behind her. She turned around and eyed me with false coyness.

"Whatcha up to?" she said. She should have been chewing gum as well as smoking.

"Good evening," I said.

"Looking for a date?"

"Yes, indeed."

"You a cop?"

"No. You?"

She laughed. "Not likely. Wanna blow job?"

I explained that I wanted something more substantial—a word that seemed to puzzle her. She said something about charging extra if I wanted anything "kinky." I suggested fifty dollars. She agreed, but still seemed worried, and wanted details. I promised that I wouldn't hurt her, and she reluctantly agreed, and said she knew a hotel nearby. Her name was Doris.

I offered her my arm. She seemed to think that was funny, but she threw her cigarette away and linked arms with me. The old world charm and fifty dollars; it never fails.

It was shortly after midnight when I led her into the lobby of the Midtown Hotel. I took a room for the evening at twenty dollars. From the look of the place, I'd have thought they were overcharging by a factor of at least two, but I didn't find out what the rooms were like, because at that moment I felt something I'd never felt before. I can say it no more clearly than that something took hold of my mind and pulled. It was disorienting, and in a way I had not thought I could be disoriented, and uncomfortable, not unlike the vertigo I felt when Young Don shot me, and again when Susan said she loved me.

Reflexes associated with panic woke up; not strong enough to interfere with me, but there, nevertheless, telling me something inexplicable was happening in my brain, where one never wants the inexplicable happening.

I was dizzy for just a moment, and my first thought was, *Kellem.* But, on reflection, it didn't feel like her. In any event, something was happening, and I was a part of it. I felt a clear sense of direction and a great sense of urgency. I took out a roll of bills and threw them at Doris, saying, "Sorry, honey, change of plans. I'll see you another time," and dashed out of the hotel. I think I remember the desk clerk laughing, and Doris swearing loudly, though whether at me or at the clerk I cannot say.

At that moment, someone said, "You are Jack Agyar." It was so strong that, for a moment, I thought it was really said into my ear and I stopped running and turned around. No, there was no one there. It had been Jill's voice, which was clearly impossible. I didn't know what this meant, but I knew that I didn't like it.

Weakness, I thought, be damned; I needed speed.

I sent myself like an arrow through the night, troubled by visions of ropes surrounding me, tying me up; at one point I was unable to move my arms, although I was able to break this without much effort. I could still hear Jill's voice, though I did not know what she was saying. I stumbled a couple of times, as if something were trying to wrap itself around my legs. At another point I stopped, realizing that, somehow, I had forgotten the way. I stood, trembling from weakness and rage, and made myself recall how I had gotten there before, and eventually I reached the correct neighborhood.

Whatever it was, it was still going on, and it was not without a certain fear that I entered the house. There was no one on the main floor, but I could smell cloth burning upstairs, and so I dashed up to Jill's room and threw open the door. She stood, naked, facing the north wall, which looked toward Susan's room and the street. Before her were small bits of cloth and yarn, a black candle, and an ashtray, in which something was burning.

She did not seem to notice me.

I rushed forward, but was stopped, as if by a wall, although there was nothing tangible in front of me. Or, more accurately, it was as if I knew I could go forward if I could make myself, and simultaneously knew I couldn't make myself. If, years from now, I am baffled when I read this, I will remind myself that I was even more baffled when it happened; I still don't understand it.

She said, "So I am free," as if speaking to someone who wasn't there, and, as she spoke, I felt a tearing sensation somewhere within me, as if a piece of myself were being ripped away.

"So I am free."

As she said it a second time, the feeling intensified, and with it my rage. I knew what was happening, although I didn't know how.

"So I am—"

"No!" I cried. That got through. She looked at me for the first time, her eyes widening. I caught her in my gaze and we struggled that way for what seemed like forever; a silent, and very deadly struggle in which, I think, neither of us was quite sure on what ground it was being fought, or how the battle was progressing, yet we were both very much aware of the conflict. *You are mine,* I told her. *You have always been mine. Your heart is mine. Your soul is mine. Your body and life are mine. Your will is a shadow of my own.*

Something, I don't know what, hung by a thread, awaiting the decision of our struggle. She was more determined than I had thought possible for her; I was as angry as I'd been in some time.

I am free, she told me. *You have no power over me.*

You are mine. You are mine.

I am free. I am free.

You are mine.

I fall back on metaphor because there is no way to set down in words what it was like, that battle of wills, a pushing and a pulling, a heating and a cooling, but that only hints at the experience like the description of the act of love can only bring fragments of the sensation to the memory.

But I was the stronger; we can, perhaps, leave it at that. Her will crumbled beneath my rage, like the unraveling of a closely knit fabric that begins to run. I took the end and pulled it, and the invisible wall before me collapsed.

She made a low sound of despair as I came forward, took her, and pushed her against the wall. "Where did you learn to do that?" I said.

She didn't answer, only made an inarticulate moan; she would have fallen if I had not been holding her.

"Tell me," I said, with all the force I could. "Tell me who and where."

She began to tremble, and there were tears running down her cheeks. Some men seem to think women are attractive when they cry; I think such men are crazy. I shook her and said, "Tell me *now.*"

In a choking, quivering voice, she told me.

"Good," I said. "Now listen to me. You are done with this forever, do you understand?"

"Yes," she whispered, not looking at me.

"You belong to me, and to me alone, do you understand?"

"I understand," she said, still trembling.

"Good. See that you don't forget."

I put my arms around her and held her very close. There were tears against my face. I was very tired; the exertions of the last two days had worn me out badly.

But I left her alive, which was, I think, more than she deserved.

I woke up feeling very old.

That is, I think that is what I am feeling. In fact, one might say that I have never been old, or that I have been old for a long time and it hasn't affected me; what I mean is, I feel the way I should imagine I would feel as an old man; there is a stiffness in the back of my knees and in my neck, I don't want to move fast, and, in general, gravity seems to have more power over me than is its wont.

And then there is the hunger, which is not a normal hunger, even for me.

I can almost touch it, it is so real. Once, in a mistake I will never make again, I spent time with a young woman who freebased cocaine. One thing, as it will, led to another, and, after only one evening with her, I could feel the craving, unlike anything I had ever felt before. Perhaps I wouldn't have been so frightened if I had felt any of the effects the drug is supposed to provide, but there was nothing at all, only the unmistakable desire for more. It wasn't strong; I had no difficulty in convincing myself to stay away from her; but I felt it, and I have never forgotten that feeling.

What I feel this morning is akin to that, only a hundred times worse. It cheapens, even humbles me, but this will in no way keep me from pursuing what I require. Indeed, I feel it a small victory over my baser instincts that I have been able to force myself to shower, brush my teeth and hair, dress carefully, have a conversation with Jim, and sit here recording all of this, so that I will know what it was like, later, after I have done what I am going to do.

I came down to the living room, and Jim was waiting for me. He looked at me closely and said, "Are you all right?"

"No," I said. "But I'll get by. I must go out."

"Be careful," he said.

There was something in his tone. I said, "Oh? Is that a general caution?"

He shook his head, looking at the pendant on my chest (which, I'm pleased to say, had not been included in the description of me). "The police have been outside all day watching the house."

"Damn them to Hell," I said.

He winced. "They've also been going through the neighborhood, asking questions."

"And showing everyone a piece of paper?"
"I didn't notice them doing that."
"Good."
"But that's not to say they weren't."
"You're just full of good news, aren't you?"
"As I said, be careful."
"I will, I will."

TWELVE

man *n.* 1. An adult male human being, as distinguished from a female. 2. Any human being, regardless of sex or age; a member of the human race; a person.

AMERICAN HERITAGE DICTIONARY

In this room where I work the typewriting machine, nothing ever changes but me. I sit here, and on one day it is warmer, on another it is colder, there is a draft or there is not, the mice are louder or quieter, the smell of decay strong or faint, but, in fact, these variations only serve to remind me that I am a viable being in a dead environment. Sometimes it seems that I am the only living thing in the world, and that it is only the products of my imagination that end up on this paper. But at other times, such as now, the aftermath of the day is too strong for such pretense.

How to begin?

At the beginning, I suppose; with walking out the door, and then try to set it all down in order, as well as I remember it. Much is hazy, but these things have a way of returning to me as I set them down.

I slipped out of the back of the house. I wasn't worried about being seen; as long as I know to be careful,

I can remain unobserved. I went across to Jefferson and down to Thirty-third, where the bus stops in front of a small privately owned neighborhood grocery store. There is a long-abandoned school across the street from it, as well as two 1920's-era houses that have not yet been abandoned. There are sometimes hookers there, too, although that is too close to my own neighborhood for my purposes. Still, had there been any girl working just then, I should not have hesitated.

In addition to buses and hookers, it is a place where cabs come by frequently. I don't like being transported, but I didn't feel that I had any choice. I had no trouble flagging one down. I climbed into the back seat and said, "Little Philly."

The driver, one of the older type (cab drivers are always younger than twenty-five or older than thirty-five; I don't know why that is), turned around and said, "You wanna be more specific than that?"

"No."

He sighed. "All right. I'll take you to Saint Thomas and Maple."

"That'll be fine," I said.

He tried to talk to me but I wasn't interested. I kept a close watch on him to see if he was going to look at me in his mirror, but he never did; else the trip would have been shorter. I paid the meter, $6.90, and tipped him two dollars and ten cents.

I spotted her almost at once; tall and black, carrying a small lavender handbag, wearing the same dark miniskirt and a brown leather coat that was too short and too light for the weather. Her expression of disdain was just like before; I guess some guys found it attractive. What was her name? Sylvia? Something like that. I took a step toward her. She saw me at about the same time, and I could feel the quick intake of her breath.

She took a step backward, looked over her shoulder

as if seeking a place to run, then turned and began walking away at a good pace. I set out after her; she ought not to be able to outrun me, even weakened as I was. Besides, I was getting desperate.

She stepped into a little cul-de-sac shopping area that was very much out of place in the neighborhood, full of flower stores, used-book stores, violin shops, and so on. I followed her through it, and out a back door into a small parking lot, probably for employees, where she stepped behind a man wearing a brown leather coat just like hers only longer and belted, checkered zip boots, and a wide-brim hat. He was thin and tough looking in a Nordic way, clean shaven and with an ugly square chin. I heard her whisper, "That's the one, Charlie. That's the man what did that thing to me."

I stared at him. "What is this?" I said. "A white pimp and a black whore? Don't you people have any respect for tradition? What if word got out?" His hand was in his pocket. When it came out I saw a glint of metal reflected from the store lights that shone on the parking lot.

I said, "Let me guess, Charlie. A butterfly knife, right?"

He said, "You know me, motherf——er?"

"You get one point for the dialogue, Charlie," I said, "but I'm afraid you lose one for the knife, and another because you're the wrong color. Sorry, net loss. Go away and try again another time. I have business with the lady. We'll call you when we're done."

She moved a little closer to him. How tender. "You f—ed with one of my girls, man." He was walking toward me as he spoke.

"I thought that was the idea."

"You're dead."

"Now there's another good line," I told him. "You just might make it on the dialogue alone. Now, do something flashy with the knife while the camera gets a close-up on your hand, okay?"

"You're pretty smart, motherf——er."

"You already called me that. Come up with something different. No, on the other hand, skip it. I want to see you make the knife do tricks." He did, too. Whoosh, whoosh, shick, shick, it went. Then he tried something even flashier, something that was supposed to hurt me. After that, he backed away, holding his right wrist in his left hand and grimacing. I threw the knife over my shoulder. It hit the plowed pavement and clanked. He gritted his teeth and reached behind him with his left hand, clumsily.

If I'd been faster, I could have prevented him from getting the gun out, but I was just too slow. It was a stupid little revolver, probably a .38, with a barrel about two inches long. But I don't like having guns pointed at me, even when I'm in the best of health.

He got off one round, which hit me low in the stomach on my right side, and that was all he had time for. Unfortunately, it gave the girl time to scream, and, worst luck of all, there turned out to be a patrol car within hearing of either the shot or the scream; the siren came almost at once.

I left him lying there and said to her, "Honey, this is your lucky day. You should find a new line of work, because I don't think you're going to have any more luck after this."

I slipped away into the night as the police arrived, leaving her to explain things however she might. My need was urgent now, painful and desperate, and the bullet wound in my stomach wasn't helping any.

There was a time when I wandered, not knowing where to go, alert as an animal for those blue uniforms. I don't know where I went, but I remember leaning against a phone booth and suddenly thinking, "I could call Susan."

I could call her, and she would come and pick me up in an automobile, and she would give me what I needed. I closed my eyes for a moment, and it seemed I could feel the heat of her skin against mine, the touch of her lips. Yes. I could call Susan, my lover, and she would come, and she would save me by—she would save me.

I pulled some coins out of my pocket and found one worth a quarter of a dollar. I let the others fall onto the floor of the phone booth; the clatter they made striking the metal floor of the telephone booth seemed inordinately loud and to echo and reverberate for a very long time.

I knew I was not well, and my hunger was a need that filled valleys and leveled mountains. Did I remember her number? Yes. I held the coin up toward the slot and noticed that my hand was shaking. That was all right; I just needed to reach Susan, and she would come for me, and take me home and—

I lurched out of the phone booth, dropping the quarter into the snow (at least, I don't have it now, and I don't remember doing anything else with it), and struggled to a place as far from any lights as possible, just because I felt the need for darkness as sanctuary. That's the real trouble with cities, much as I love them: there's nowhere that is truly dark.

There was a sweep of headlights past me, and for a moment I thought it was the police again, but no. I was on the ground floor of a parking ramp, in the corner away from the little booth and the exit and entrance.

Parking ramps are dangerous places.

I looked around for video cameras and didn't see one. Then I waited. I couldn't afford to be choosy this time, it was a matter of survival. Any age, any sex, as

long as he or she was alone; I didn't think I could survive
a serious conflict of any kind.

I waited.

I huddled with myself, and the cold, though it could
not penetrate the ugly parka, found all of the niches in
the sleeves and collar. I shivered, and my teeth chattered.
No one came, and no one came, and then a group of
four, then two couples, and then no one and no one and
no one. The sliver of moon had set many hours before.

Me, too.

Bars were closing, and now there were too many
people. I waited, desperate and shivering, and my body
clock went tick . . . tick . . . tick, winding down. People
everywhere, walking past; cars starting, leaving, jockey-
ing for position in the rush to the exit. A young couple
whose Toyota was parked directly in front of me got into
their car, and the man seemed to see me, but looked
away. He probably thought I was drunk. Maybe he
thought I was going to freeze to death and didn't care.
What's become of human decency?

Tick . . . tick . . . tick.

Not so many, now. Footsteps echo through the
empty ramp, but always in pairs.

Tick . . . tick . . . tick.

Now, no one at all.

Is it over? There are still a few cars, but perhaps they
are abandoned.

Should I return home? Can I make it home at all?

Patience, patience. There is all eternity before you.

Tick . . . tick . . . tick.

Could I bring Jill to me? That would be better than
nothing. But no, I could see the ugly beige partitions
through her unfocused eyes, feel the needle in her arm,
hear the rolling of carts down a hospital corridor. She
would never make it here.

Tick . . . tick . . . tick.

Footsteps.

Another couple; the man very drunk, and large, from the sound of his footfalls, a woman with him, telling him that she'll drive. He is arguing. I must take a chance, because there may not be anyone else. Besides, she is right; he ought not to be on the road tonight; what if he killed someone?

They walked past my spot, about thirty feet from me, and I fell in behind them. My legs were very stiff from having squatted there by the wall for so long, but I was no longer cold. He would be likely to fight, whereas she would be likely to scream. Of course, you cannot tell these days; it could be the other way around, but I went with the probabilities. A fight would be bad, a scream would be worse.

Now they were at their car, an old Dodge Dart that looked like he'd driven it drunk once or twice already. They were standing by the door, still arguing about who was going to drive. He was being stubborn. Maybe I could take them both at once, and not have to worry about either a fight or a scream. That would be best. I resolved to try, in any case.

I approached them; she on my right, he on my left. I'd have preferred it the other way around, but you take what you can get. I braced myself. It was going to have to be quick and certain.

I said, "Excuse me." They turned as I approached. The woman seemed to be in her early forties, with blue-gray eyes, and so muffled that I could tell little else about her. The man was about the same age, and, indeed, large; perhaps six feet tall and husky. I guessed most of his weight to be fat, but I've been wrong before.

He scowled at me and said, "Whattaya want?"

Afterward I leaned against the car, closed my eyes, and knew that I would live. I'd been right: mostly fat. When I was a few blocks away I went through the wallet and the purse. I can give them a name now: Lawrence and Roberta Tailor. His wallet had her picture in it, and another picture showing two girls, aged about five and seven; daughters, I suppose, but that wasn't what I was looking for. I found the money and the credit cards, and threw everything else in a Dumpster. Just another typical robbery-murder, folks. Nothing to get excited about. Probably a gang. We need law and order, don't you think? Most likely drug related. Just say no.

On my way home I threw the credit cards in the river. The money I kept. What the Hell.

I'm feeling better, although not as good as I'd like. I'm sorry that I had to kill Lawrence, but I didn't really have any choice. I don't feel bad about Roberta because I didn't kill her; the embalmers will do that. A shame, but it isn't my problem.

Today's lesson: Everything is relative.

I don't think I'm really in any better health than I was when I rose yesterday, but, after all I went through, I don't mind so much.

Jim didn't notice the difference. "You look rough," he said.

"I have a right to. It was grim last night."

"Oh?"

"For starters, I was shot."

He was suddenly very concerned. "Where?"

"Stomach."

"Bad?"

"It could have been worse; there could have been sunshine."

"Do you need anything?"

"I should be all right, now. I just have to give it some time."

"Tell me what happened."

I did. He listened, looking past my shoulder. When I was done, he said, "What are you going to do?"

"Recover. I'll take my time about it, though; I'll be careful."

He chuckled. "You're learning wisdom. It's about time."

I shrugged. He didn't have anything else to say, so I came up to my little typewriting sanctuary, thinking that I would feel better after speaking to this machine, but now I find I don't have anything to talk about.

I think I can risk seeing Susan today.

She continues to amaze me. Every time I am with her, it is like a renewal. I am challenged in mind and spirit, and filled with an indefinable desire for higher things. And yet, there is nothing magical about it, unless, indeed, human romantic love is magic, which might be true; I wouldn't know, not being a poet save now and again when I can't help myself.

The clouds were low, with a bright quarter-moon, still low in the east, providing backlighting for some unusual cumulus formations—the ice-cream cone variety, with puffy mounds on top tapering down almost to a point. I didn't think they would dump any snow on us before tomorrow. The air was a bit warm and full of moisture and the smells of man and nature, who keep changing each other and producing queer odors while doing so.

The blue lights were still on in the attic, giving me the pleasant feeling that all was as it should be. I knocked on the door. Music that I didn't recognize was turned down, there was the slap of Susan's bare feet against the floor, and she opened the door.

The first thing she said was, "Do you know about Jill?"

"What about her?"

"She's in the hospital."

I pretended surprise, widening my eyes and leaning against the wall. "A relapse?"

She nodded. She was wearing a big pink furry bathrobe and her hair was set and slicked back; she smelled fresh, clean, and entirely wholesome. Her eyes were wide, and she looked at me as if I were the only thing in the world. "I went in to her room this morning and she was chalky white, and gasping, like she could hardly breath. I thought she might have pneumonia, or had suddenly become asthmatic."

"You called 911?"

"Yes. They gave her oxygen and took her away."

"Sounds very frightening."

"It was. I'm all right now, but I wish you'd been here."

"So do I. What have you heard?"

"From the hospital? Nothing yet."

"Hmmm. I'll have to bring her some flowers."

"She'd like that," said Susan. Then she frowned suddenly and looked at me as if seeing me for the first time. "Are you all right?"

"Sure. Why?"

"You look, I don't know, *hunted.*"

That shook me a bit; I'm not used to people being quite so perspicacious. I said, "I'm a little short on sleep, I guess." I forced a laugh and took my coat off. "I hope I don't have what Jill has."

She took it seriously. "You *do* look a bit pale, and sort of wan."

"Hmmm."

We sat on the couch together. She said, "What happened to your other coat?"

"It's being cleaned. Isn't that thing hideous?"

"In a word: yes. But on the other hand, there isn't much winter left."

"True."

"Would you like some wine?"

"No, thank you."

"You don't drink much, do you?"

"I drink deeply of your eyes, my love."

She laughed and took my hand that was about her shoulders, caressed it, pressed it against her face. Her face was very warm. We sat like that for several minutes.

I said, "To whom are we listening?"

"Kate Bush."

"She sounds Irish."

"She is."

She fell silent—Susan, that is, not Kate Bush. The latter continued to sing. She's good, if you like that sort of thing. I thought I might, in another fifty years or so.

I could feel that Susan was deep in thought; I remained silent, enjoying her touch, knowing that eventually she would tell me what was on her mind. After two or three minutes she said, "Jonathan."

"Yes?"

"If I stop seeing Jennifer, will you stop seeing Jill?"

I looked at her, my mouth suddenly dry. I said, "You continue to astound me."

"I hope that's good," she said.

"That's good."

"But what is your answer?"

I kissed her, then went on kissing her. After a while I picked her up and carried her upstairs, where I held her close for a long time before doing anything else.

I reached a place, but did she reach it with me? Can I know? It seems she did, but I am capable of lying to myself. It seemed that we were where touch was deeper than touch, where the physical paths we led each other along made all of the base mechanics of lovemaking more than irrelevant; a place few are privileged to visit, and those few only rarely; a place where, once you've been there, you might spend the rest of your life in a futile effort to get back to. It is for this reason that pleasure must always have at least this element of risk, if no other: That perhaps this joy will never occur again. But this serpent will invade only the loveliest, most bountiful gardens; his presence in such gardens is inevitable, and we accept it serenely, and with gratitude, for we know that we have been privileged.

So, at least, were my thoughts as I lay in bed next to my lover, who slept with a smile on her face that brought an ache to my heart and a tear to my eye.

I tried to remember what it had been like with Laura. I remembered the intensity, the need, and the feeling that she shared it, but little else. I remembered a few occasions—most of them moments while we walked, she would clasp me to her, and there would be the feeling of growing and diminishing, and then I'd walk on, my knees shaking, feeling weak, distant, confused, but vaguely triumphant. But that is all. Certainly, I could recall nothing that would make me think love could change how the act itself felt. Wouldn't it be funny if, so long ago, she had been in love, and I'd only been fooling myself?

What a silly thing to wonder about.

I lay next to Susan and rested, and thought about nothing at all.

Some hours later she stirred. I kissed the palm of her hand and said, "Are you awake?"

"Mmmm. A little."

"Are you awake enough to answer a question?"

She stretched and shifted. "If it's an easy one."

"Oh. Well, never mind."

She opened her eyes, squinted at me, licked her lips. When she is awake, her sheet and comforter are always waist-high, which I'm certain she does on purpose, because Susan doesn't do things like that accidentally. "What is it?" she said.

I caressed her hair and the side of her face. "Tell me something, then."

"Hmmmm?"

"What's it like for you?"

"What do you mean, 'it'?"

"When we make love. What's it like?"

She smiled a Susan smile, full of light. "Fishing for compliments, are we?"

"No."

She tilted her head. "You look so serious."

"I get that way sometimes. What's it like?"

"It's nice. It's sort of dreamy and romantic, all warm and soft and red."

"Red?"

"Mmmm."

"I don't know what you mean."

"I'm not sure I do either. Is it important?"

I sighed. "I guess not. Sleep now, my love."

"Mmmm," she said, and did.

It has been several days since I have set anything down on paper. There has been little enough to tell; I have been resting and recovering. I have spoken to Susan over the telephone, but I've been afraid to see her for fear of what I might do. I sent Jill flowers, and I have been gathering strength; slowly, but quickly enough. Today I am feeling almost myself again.

I spent today reading over some of what I've written on this typewriting machine, and I'm struck by all the things that, for some reason or another, I have never recorded. I didn't mention that business with the cab driver that almost got me in trouble, I said nothing about the fight in the back room of Flannery's that led me to decide not to go back there, or how I fought with a van and won (that was amusing; I wish I could remember it better) and nothing at all about Susan's birthday party and the scene Jill made.

All of which leads me to wonder at the subconscious processes by which I decide what I ought to set down. It's a shame, too, because there are things that I think I won't remember, and would appreciate having recorded. I wish I'd thought of doing this years ago; perhaps I'd remember what Paris was like, and I think I'd get a smile out of my recollections of Kiri-chan.

I also noticed, as I read, that my selection of detail seems to have changed in the few scant months since I began these pages, as if before I wished to note the passing of words between me and others, and now it is the deeds, and especially the blood, that have taken hold of my mind. Why is that? If it implies a change in me, I don't think it is a change for the better.

Or maybe it isn't really a change at all; maybe most of what I've recorded are things that, in one way or another, surprised me; there are certainly enough of these. I didn't think Kellem would want to destroy me, I didn't think I'd be unable to deduce what she had done that worried her so, I didn't think a woman could have the kind of effect on me that Susan has had, and I certainly didn't think Jill would be able to come so close to breaking away from me.

Which reminds me of some unfinished business. I must find a dilapidated hotel called the Hollywood that, according to Jill, is on Foster just outside of Little Philly, and I must gain entrance to the boarding house next door, and I must have a talk with the woman who has been plaguing me more than Kellem has.

Now that I think of it, Kellem has done nothing since the time the police visited the house; and come to that, why am I so certain Kellem arranged for the visit? It might have been the old woman's doing, or maybe something completely unrelated. Maybe, with one thing and another, I've cut my own throat, without the need for Kellem to do anything at all; that would be true irony. But still, why would she need to be so subtle when all she would have had to do is command me to do something and I would have been required to obey, just as

Just as Jill is.

By my lost grace, could it be? Is such a thing possible?

THIRTEEN

pur·pose *n*. 1. The object toward which one strives or for which something exists; goal; aim. 2. A result or effect that is intended or desired; intention. 3. Determination; resolution. 4. The matter at hand; point at issue.

AMERICAN HERITAGE DICTIONARY

The church bells, unusual for a Friday, finally stopped several hours ago. I think by now it must be Saturday morning. March has all but ended, but it still feels like mid-February; I'm tempted to take this as a personal affront.

Once more, now, I am feeling well and fit, as if the trials of a week ago had not occurred, save for the wounds of experience, which bring strength, not weakness. I found a telephone and spoke to Jill in the hospital, and wished her a speedy recovery. They do not, she said, have any idea what happened to her, but she says she's doing well. They were concerned that she had attempted suicide at first, but not any more. She expects to return home within a day or two.

I can relax now, and consider the impossible, and prepare for exertions to come, for there may be some. The notion does not frighten me. If I am correct in my surmises (why do I want to say surmisi?), then I will still carry out the visit I had intended to make, only I will do so with a different purpose. This, I think, will happen tomorrow.

If I am right, then I can leave this place, and never need to worry about Kellem again. Perhaps, even, Susan will come with me; I should like that very much. But I dare not broach the subject until I have some reason to believe I will escape this peril.

Before, the notion of opposing Kellem was unthinkable. Now, all of a sudden, I can not only consider it, but I have, indeed, been thinking of little else for the past several days, even to the point of failing in my duty to this machine. The notion fills me with an excitement such as I have never felt; one that is not unmixed with fear, but is no less strong for that.

I am not weary, but sleep is, nevertheless, coming on. Tomorrow, more will occur.

I have this odd piece of paper in front of me. I read it, and I wonder if I have been made a fool of. I hope not. I think not. Unless something happens to change my mind, I will assume not.

When I left the house it was early in the evening, the full moon had not yet risen, and I was greeted by the aftermath of a freezing rain; one of those ambiguous signs that either says, "It will be colder soon," or, "It will be warmer before too long." For the time of year, it ought to be the latter, but I am not convinced. But it makes the streets and sidewalks just as slippery either way, and everywhere I saw the flashing lights of tow trucks doing their job and policemen too busy to look for the likes of me.

In spite of the fact that I walked all the way—treading, as it were, on thin ice—it was still early when I found the hotel, every bit as ugly as I'd been told, with red brick and a cracked glass door next to a revolving door that bore an "out of order" sign that seemed very old. I looked at the other doors that were a part of the same structure, and one of them had, drawn in chalk, a circle with a dot in the middle of it. Inside the door, a public hallway, were three mailboxes. I recognized the name on number two.

There were three doors on the landing at the top of the long, narrow stairway. The one I wanted was not difficult to identify; it was in the middle and had a number on it, albeit hanging upside down from one nail. It also had her name above the door in glittering letters.

I knocked upon the door and waited.

There was the sound of shuffling feet, and the door was opened as far as the security chain would permit. I found myself regarding a pair of dark eyes cast into an old, weathered face poured from a mold I'd seen many times in many places. The eyes regarded me, widened, narrowed, then appeared to consider. I had the feeling that I'd been recognized.

After a moment the door closed, the chain slipped off, and the door opened again; apparently she realized that such devices are neither sufficient nor necessary. She supported herself with a wooden stick in one hand, the other gripping the door.

Her voice was sharp and brittle. She said. "You must be John Agyar."

"Yes," I said. "Good evening."

She nodded, watching me carefully.

I said, "Are you going to invite me in?"

"No."

"Ah. Then we must converse this way?"

"I have nothing to say to you. What have you to say to me? I'm too old for threats to mean anything."

"I'll bet you say that to all the guys."

"Only for as long as it's been true. What do you want?"

"I thought you could tell me my future."

She snorted. "My crystal ball isn't here. What do you want?"

I shrugged. "I dislike standing by the door. Can we meet somewhere?"

"Do you think I'm so foolish?"

"Au contraire, as my friend the ghost likes to say. I believe you are wise enough to take precautions, and intelligent enough to know what precautions to take. As it happens, I have no desire to harm you in any way; but I am wise enough not to expect you to believe me and intelligent enough to invite any reasonable alternative."

She stared at me for a moment more, looking me dead in the eye as if to tell me I could do nothing to her, which may even have been true. Then she nodded. "There is a cafe in the hotel downstairs; I'll meet you there."

"I'll wait for you outside."

She snorted a little. "Very well. I will see you in a moment."

I returned to the street and found a dark place to await the redoubtable lady and keep an eye out for the police, just in case she thought to call them on me. I decided that I liked her; I hoped I wouldn't have to kill her.

Twenty minutes later she came out of the door, helped by two walking sticks. She was heavily muffled against the weather, wearing a dark wool coat and a matching hat and scarf, thick woolen mittens with little metal clasps attaching them to her coat sleeves, such as children wear so they don't lose their mittens. I suspect that she had made most of the items herself.

She looked around for me and I stepped up next to her. She didn't jump; she just scowled and said, "Come along." She didn't have much trouble walking in spite of the icy sidewalk, I suppose because of years of practice and the shortness of her steps. A boy of about eighteen was spreading salt on the sidewalk as we walked by, but it hadn't started working yet.

I followed her into the cafe, which consisted of about ten green plastic booths and some stools arranged in a long rectangle. The interior decoration was chrome, except for additional aesthetic statements provided by the coats hanging on racks which were attached to the end of each booth; patrons sitting at the counter were, I suppose, expected to leave their coats on.

It was just past the dinner hour, so, while there was no one in line ahead of us, we had to wait almost five minutes for them to clean off a table; five minutes which my companion spent complaining loudly about being made to wait standing. A harried-looking but not unattractive middle-aged waitress offered her a seat at the counter while she waited, an offer that was declined with a sniff.

At last we were shown to a booth. I helped her with her coat, removed my own; I saw from the thin gold chains around her neck that my companion, who wore a severe black dress, had not neglected anything; we sat down. The silver was ugly, and set on a paper place mat full of pictures of covered bridges; it had been printed by the Lakota tourist bureau and should have been called, "What to avoid in Ashtabula County."

My dinner partner propped her canes against the booth, and set her purse next to her. She picked up the one-page plastic menu from behind the napkin holder, glanced at it, and said, "Well? The beef stew is good. Or perhaps some chili since the day is so cold?"

"Funny," I said. "Thanks just the same, I think I'll pass this time."

She sniffed, replaced the menu, and folded her hands in front of her. She said, "No doubt. Well, then, let's get on with it. What do you want?"

"Coffee?" said the waitress, coming up behind me.

"Please," I said. "Half a cup."

"Tea," said my companion. "With lemon."

The waitress went away, and came back presently with a little tin of hot water and a bag of Lipton's. She poured me half a cup of coffee, learned that I didn't need cream, and was informed that we would not be ordering food, which didn't seem to bother her. She went away.

The old woman put the tea bag in the thick ceramic cup and poured the water over it, scowling as if it had offended her in some way. "What do you want from me?" she said.

"As I said, I want to know my future."

"You know your future as well as I do; the only question is when, and you are aware, I think, that I would not tell you that even if I could. What do you want?"

So much for polite conversation. I said, "You know who Jill Quarrier is."

"Of course."

"Then you ought to know that she failed."

The old woman frowned. "Failed?"

"She didn't have what it took."

"She couldn't have—"

"If I had left her alone, it might have been different. Then again, it might not have."

She glared at me. "What have you done to her?"

"She lives."

"How do you mean that?"

"As you do. She breathes, her heart beats, she eats and drinks and tells jokes."

The old woman sniffed. "Well?"

"Well, I want to know how she did it."

She scowled at me. After a moment, she said, "What's the difference? It failed."

"It failed because, as I said, she didn't have what it

took after I interrupted the proceedings. I do, no matter
who interrupts me."

"You?"

"Yes."

"I don't understand."

"It isn't necessary that you understand. I am bound
in a certain way by a certain person. I wish to free myself.
I didn't think it could be done, but you and Jill have
shown me that I am wrong."

"How? If—"

"She came very close."

"I see."

She sipped at her tea, glared at it, then glared at me.
"Why should I help you?" she said.

"Jill Quarrier," I said.

She frowned. "I don't understand."

"She is mine. I own her. I can do what I will to her.
After her attempt to escape me, I put her in the hospital.
I can do so again. And again. Eventually, I will have all
of her."

"You—"

"She is expected to get out tomorrow or the next
day."

Her mouth worked up and down, without ever closing completely. If looks could kill and so on. "I can put
such protections on her that—"

"Against her will?"

"What do you mean, against her will?"

"I mean against my will. Think about it."

She did so, grinding her teeth. I wondered if they
were real. After a long time, she took another sip of tea,
forgetting even to scowl at it. At length, she said, "What
exactly are you offering?"

"Jill. Her life, her health, her freedom."

"In exchange for telling you how to break free from
whoever is binding you?"

"Exactly."

"How do I know you will keep your end of the bargain?"

"You don't. But you know what will happen to Jill if you refuse."

"It will happen anyway," she snapped. "And you know it—"

"Rubbish. If I release her, and leave her alone, she will live a full and normal life."

"Yes, until she dies."

"We're all in for that eventually."

"But when *she* dies—"

"She will be embalmed. Or maybe cremated."

Her mouth worked again, this time from side to side, as if she were having trouble with her teeth. "What is it you want to be released from?"

"The same as Jill."

She stared at me. "I have lived for many years, and I have seen my share of evil, but—"

"Spare me."

"Spare you? How amusing. Perhaps someday you will beg me for exactly that."

"Not likely," I said. "And it might not be clever of you to make me think that I would rest easier with you dead."

"I don't fear you."

"The lady doth protest too much, methinks."

She snorted. "And the Devil is quoting Shakespear."

"Oh, hardly the Devil, I think."

"The servant is the man."

I laughed a little and played with my coffee cup. I said, "You know, I think, that I am not deliberately cruel."

"I know nothing of the kind."

"Then you should know it. Because I can be cruel if

I want to be, if I see a need to be. If you think of betraying me in any way, you should consider it carefully. Whatever you do to me, I will take out on Jill, and I will show you what I have done to her before I do the same to you. It would be good of you to consider this."

"Don't threaten me, monster. I do what I promise."

I laughed. "Tell it to the air, *cigány;* I know your kind. But I think you will this time." I repressed a chuckle, suddenly remembering how Young Don had interpreted that word he didn't recognize.

She glared at me again. "You'd best find paper and pencil to write this down; it is long."

"Very well." I signaled the waitress over. She asked if we wanted anything else. I asked for a pen. She provided one and went away again. I turned over the place mat and prepared to write.

The old woman said, "It must be done under the waning moon, the new moon is best."

"Very well."

"And you must begin at midnight."

I laughed.

"You think it's a joke?" she snapped.

"Of course. But that doesn't mean I won't do it."

Her mouth twitched angrily and she began speaking. I wrote it all down. The paper was too coarse. I prefer typing, I think.

I have typewritten the instructions and set them aside until the moon should become newer. Why is it that we call the moon new when we can't see her at all? For that matter, why do we say first quarter or third quarter when any fool can see it is a half-moon? Now, by the way, she is big and full and beautiful, rising early in the evening and setting as the sun rises.

I walked through the bitter cold that might be winter's last serious effort for the year. The harsh winds, I am told, come from Lake Erie and make their way into the center of the state where they become mild and people complain of the cold. Those from Lakota consider themselves hardy, superior folk for surviving winters with winds like this; I think, perhaps, they are merely stupid; and I am including Laura Kellem in their number. I will not stay here a moment beyond the time I am bound; a time which will, I think, end in two weeks, at the dark of the moon of April.

But what if Susan wants to stay? Will I remain here in spite of the risks? No, not unless there is a way to protect myself from Kellem—protect myself thoroughly. And, of course, there is such a way. It makes me tremble to contemplate it, but it is not impossible. If it is that or leave Susan, well, it may become more reasonable. Or not. If I can free myself from Kellem, that is enough; she is stronger than I, and older, and, even if I owed her no gratitude, it would be foolish to take such a risk.

It is funny, I think, how I cannot conceive of life without Susan, and yet we've never talked about such things. Or perhaps we have—that she offered to give up her other lover is, I think, as unprecedented for her as these feelings are for me.

I believe I will go see her, and maybe we will talk about these things, and perhaps I will be in for another shock—an unpleasant one if my suppositions prove to be ill-founded. But it is better to know than not to know, isn't it?

I spent the evening with Susan, though we didn't go anywhere and I didn't touch her, save for an arm around her shoulder. She seemed disappointed, and I was sad that I couldn't explain.

We sat on her couch listening to Maazel conduct the Cleveland Orchestra through Shostakovich's Symphony

Number 5. I've always liked Shostakovich; he's morbid.
I said, "Jill isn't back yet, is she?"

"No. I spoke to her, and she said she'd be getting
out tomorrow. Are you going to be here to welcome
her?"

"I don't know."

"Perhaps you should."

"Yes. And then, perhaps I shouldn't."

She said, "You know, Jonathan, you never actually
said that you'd stop seeing Jill if I stopped seeing Jennifer."

"I implied it pretty strongly, though."

She smiled and nestled closer to me. "Mmmm," she
said.

"But all right, I formally agree. Yes. Done. Com-
pact made, signed, and sealed. An alliance offensive and
defensive against this wicked world."

"That will do," she said.

"I will tell her next time I see her."

She frowned, watched me with her big eyes, and
said, "Do you think that right after she comes out of the
hospital is the best time?"

"Somehow," I said, "I don't think it will break her
heart."

"Oh?"

"Trust me."

"I do."

"When are you going to tell Jennifer?"

She nestled her head against my shoulder and said,
"About two hours ago."

"Oh. Hmmm. How did she take it?"

"She's a bit of a bitch. But we're going to get together and talk things over."

I almost offered to make sure she stayed out of her
life, but then I thought that she wouldn't like that. My
next idea was that I could simply cause her to disappear,

but then Susan might feel guilty about it. Perhaps I ought to just allow things to run their course. I'm glad I didn't send that letter to Traci.

I said, "Confident, weren't you?"

"Yes." She stroked my hair.

"But," I said.

"Yes? But?"

"What of the future?"

She pulled her head back just a little and looked at me. "What of it?"

"I have been considering leaving this city."

"Oh," she said, very carefully.

"If I do, will you come with me?"

She frowned. "I'm not sure. I'll have to think about it. Everything I've been working for—"

"I know. You don't have to decide now, just think about it."

"All right."

"If you decide to stay, I might not be able to leave."

"Is it so important that you do?"

"I don't know. It might be."

"Why?"

I shook my head and we listened to the music. Susan never presses me about things; that is one thing I like about her. After a while I said, "You never press me about things; that is one thing I like about you."

"Mmmm. What's another."

"Your body."

"You're batting a thousand so far, cutie pie. What else?"

"How shy and hesitant you are about discussing your own merits."

She laughed that wonderful laugh. "I was wondering when you were going to get to that."

Outside, the sky wheeled above us, and the full moon sank in the west.

* * *

I guess I'll never make a detective.

I have this whole pile of information from the newspaper, and I couldn't find what I wanted. Why? Because I was looking the wrong way. I was trying to find something that said, "Laura Kellem committed this murder," knowing, really, that even had she signed her work the signature wouldn't have made it into the paper. If, instead, I'd looked at it the other way around, I would have seen it at once.

And if I'd known what was going on, I could have been more circumspect, and then—but what's the point? I might as well record it as it happened, and save the reflections, if any, for later.

I came downstairs today after my shower and found Jim staring out the remains of the one window that both faced front and wasn't boarded up. I said, "Are they still out there?"

"I'm not sure," he said. "But they have been here, off and on, every day for the last week."

"So they probably aren't neglecting us at night, either."

He nodded and turned to face me; or, rather, the wall over my right shoulder.

I went up to the window, looked out, and swore under my breath so I wouldn't upset Jim. "What are they after? Is it those two assholes I killed?"

"Maybe," said Jim. "They frown on other people killing drug dealers; I imagine they think it presumptuous."

"Narrow of them." I continued to stare out the window, trying to see if anyone was out there. At last I gave up and stared morosely at the hearth. "I suppose starting a fire is right out," I said.

"Do you think it's Laura Kellem?" he said.

I didn't answer; I just didn't know any more. And I

didn't know if the police had the house under constant surveillance, or just periodic drive-bys.

I put my horrible coat on. Jim said, "Where are you going?"

"I want to see how our police force is spending my tax dollars."

"You don't pay taxes."

"I'll see you later."

He licked his lips. Why would a ghost lick his lips? "Be careful," he said.

"Yes."

I left the way I was getting used to leaving—carefully, over roofs, and with darkness all around me. Having got that far, I checked out the area and found them very quickly, half a block down the street: Two gentlemen sitting in a running car drinking coffee while passing a pair of binoculars back and forth. Just like in the movies. Did the Lakota police have the manpower to spare for twenty-four-hour surveillance like this? Apparently, unless I just happened to catch them. Or maybe Mel Gibson had said, "Look, Captain, I just know that place is it. Let me check it out." And Robert Duvall had said, "We can't spare you. How are you coming on the Johnson embezzlement case?" And Mel had said, "Captain, I've got three weeks of vacation built up, and I'm taking them right now." Then a quick cut to exterior house, background, car parked down the block, foreground, two men in car—

No, not very likely. Sorry, Mel.

They knew I was about, and they knew I frequented the house, and they were watching for me. Why?

I looked around a little more, but they seemed to be the only ones. The thought came that I could do for them both right then, but, to put it mildly, it would not have helped the situation.

Then another thought came to me, and, after some

reflection, I could see no problem with it. I positioned myself behind a tree, cloaked in the night, and I waited. The moon, waning from the full, rose in the heavens.

After a time, I knew that one of the policemen was sleeping, and the other, the passenger, was staring straight ahead. I walked up to the car and tapped on the window. The driver was of middle years, perhaps forty or forty-five, and had a flat face of the type that makes one think he was dropped on it as a child. He didn't look anything like Mel Gibson. The passenger looked like Robert Duvall. He stared at me without expression and without blinking, and rolled down the window.

I said, "Why are you here?"

"Orders," he said. Ask a stupid question . . .

I said, "For whom are you watching?"

"Homicide suspect," he said. His voice was wheezy. He probably smoked too much; the noxious odor of secondhand smoke wafted from the car along with warm air from the heater.

"Does this homicide suspect have a name?"

"John Agyar, alias Jack Agyar, alias Yanosh Agyar."

Now was not the time to attempt to get into the Guinness Book for endurance cursing, nor was it the time to correct his pronunciation of my name. I said, "How do you know he lives there?"

Robert Duvall's face contorted just a bit because I had made him think; he probably had to put together things he had been directly told with things he'd happened to hear. He said, "A neighbor identified the sketch, and his em oh matches two homicides that happened there."

I didn't know what an "em oh" was, but I got the idea. I said, "Give me the sketch."

He did. His companion, the driver who didn't resemble Mel Gibson, started snoring. I looked at the sketch; this one was considerably better. It mentioned the coat again, and also included the pendant, damn it.

"Here, put this back."

He did so.

I said, "Are you sure the drug dealers were killed by Agyar?"

He said, "Yes."

"Why?"

"Same kind of killing as the other two, and maybe three more."

"All right—wait. Other *two?*"

"Yes."

Literal son of a bitch. "What others? Name them."

"Kowalczek and Swaggart, maybe the Tailors, and maybe a pimp named Alvin Jorgenson, alias Charlie George."

"Say those names again."

"Kowalczek, Swaggart, Tailor, Tailor, and Jorgenson."

Ah ha.

I said, "Who was Kowalczek?"

"Theresa Kowalczek, female Caucasian, aged twenty-four."

"How did she die?"

"Her throat was ripped out."

"That was never in the papers," I said. He didn't say anything, and I realized I hadn't asked a question. "Why wasn't that in the papers?"

"It was hushed up."

"By whom?"

"Baldy."

"Baldy?"

"Yes."

"Who is Baldy?"

"Theodore Baldwin."

I clucked my tongue and tried again. "Who is Theodore Baldwin?"

"The mayor of Lakota."

The mayor?

"What does the mayor have to do with this?"

"His son was engaged to Terri Kowalczek."

Oh, Kellem, good work. "What is known about the killing?"

"Some sort of love triangle. This Agyar was involved with one or the other of them, either Kowalczek or Baldwin, we don't know which."

Probably pretty accurate, if one were to substitute Kellem for Agyar. "Hasn't someone—umm. What is Baldwin's first name?"

"Brian."

"Hasn't someone asked Brian Baldwin?"

"He isn't saying anything, and he's been sick."

"Sick how?"

"I don't know; that's what we've heard."

"Is he in the hospital?"

"Yes."

"Where?"

"I don't know."

Unfortunately, it all made sense. "When did the investigation break?"

"When Donald Swaggart was killed the same way, and we got a witness."

"What is known about this Agyar?"

"Nothing, except that he's been seen in this neighborhood, both before and after the bodies were found in the house."

I wondered how my dear neighbor Bill would feel if he were to wake up one morning and find his wife dead. My musings were interrupted by the radio, which had being going pretty continuously, starting to sound urgent. It occurred to me that my friends had been out of

touch for a while, and it was always possible that someone would call or drive by to check on them, if they
hadn't done so already.

Robert Duvall was still looking at me, waiting. He
would continue to do so for some time, unless he was told
to do something different.

"Now listen to me," I said.

"Yes."

"There must be something wrong with the exhaust
system in this car."

"Yes."

"You have had the engine running, and you both
fell asleep."

"Yes."

"In a moment, you will spill your coffee on your lap,
and that will wake you up."

"Yes."

"You will know at once that you have passed out
from carbon monoxide poisoning, and you will roll down
the window, turn the car off, and wake up your partner."

"Yes."

"First you will roll up the window, and you will
forget doing so, and you will forget this conversation
entirely, then you will spill your coffee."

"Yes."

"Do so now."

He rolled up his window and I got out of there.

I returned to the house, came up to my typing room,
and dug through the sheaf of papers that my friend from
the newspaper had given me, and it was all there, between
the lines; hints of a love triangle, hints of a gruesome
death, if you were looking for them. The whole thing was
there. The trouble was, I'd been looking for the gruesome
death part, rather than trying to spot a murder that made
so much noise Kellem would know it couldn't be hushed
up.

Yes, indeed, the fool had fallen for the mayor's son, and, when his fiancée had refused to back out quietly, Kellem had gone off her head and killed her. Idiot. And, on top of it all, Kellem wouldn't leave. Why? I suppose because she was in love with him. Double idiot.

Hmmm. Of course, if Kellem is in love, that might explain why I

Never mind. My own feelings require no explanation. Nor do my actions.

But it all makes sense, I think. I now know the situation, and how I've been put into the middle of it. The police are watching the house, they will probably search it again, and eventually some fine morning someone will notice something funny about the bookcase or the dimensions of the basement, and then they will either locate the catch or simply bash down the wall, and then they will find me, and then—

And I'm stuck here, because that stupid bitch Kellem won't let me leave.

Now, at any rate, I know the cure for that. I must take it soon.

FOURTEEN

i·de·al *n.* 1. A conception of something in its absolute perfection. 2. One regarded as a standard or model of perfection. 3. An ultimate object of endeavor; a goal. 4. An honorable or worthy principle or aim. 5. That which exists only in the mind.

AMERICAN HERITAGE DICTIONARY

Maybe I will make a good detective after all; I seem to have developed the knack of finding what I want through sheer, boring drudgework, which, as I understand it, is most of what detectives do. In this case, I called every hospital in the area asking to speak with Brian Baldwin. The first one I tried was University Hospital on Jefferson, where Jill was staying, because that would have made things sweet and easy, but I had no such luck. In any case, it wouldn't have mattered, because I learned that she had been discharged that morning. So I got a telephone directory and started making calls. Eighteen times I asked to speak with Brian Baldwin; eighteen times I was asked if he was an inpatient; eighteen times I said yes; eighteen times I was told, very apologetically, that he didn't seem to be listed and was I certain of the spelling of his name; the nineteenth I was told that it was too late to ring the patient rooms.

The hospital is called Saint Matthew's, and it is

located outside of town in one of the high-class suburbs. Now, I must tackle the problem of gaining entry. I don't—yes, in fact, I do know how to go about it. More later.

Some time ago I dated an Emergency Room nurse, and I learned about some of the odder things that happen in hospital emergency rooms.

For example, once a patient had, somehow, gotten a lightbulb stuck in his, um, rectal passage, without breaking it, and to remove it the crew found a lamp, screwed the lamp into the lightbulb, and pulled it out. In another case, someone managed to get himself stuck in a stairwell, drunk, and wearing almost nothing. Since this was in a warm climate, no one thought of hypothermia, so when CPR failed he was pronounced dead, and the intern was breaking the news to the family when his heart started beating again. There was another case where a man had gotten a four-inch-thick piece of steel tubing driven through his chest—a piece that was too long to fit into the elevator, so they had to walk him up the stairway to surgery. He lived.

And here's another example, from right here in Lakota, that happened just a few hours ago.

A man was found lying flat on his back outside of the Emergency Room entrance. A quick check indicated no pulse and no respiration. He was brought in and CPR was administered, as well as adrenaline injections (they will never know how much he enjoyed that), but, after twenty minutes, there was no response. They disconnected him, covered him over, and wheeled him out into the hall. Eventually, when those who come for bodies came for him he was gone. While they were trying to track him down, they found an ER admissions nurse who said that he had walked by her, winked, and disappeared down the hall toward the administrative section.

Some time later, an ob-gyn nurse was found, dazed and pale, slumped against her desk. Maybe someone thought to ask her if she'd seen the fellow, and maybe she looked puzzled, nodded, and passed out. More likely, the incidents were never connected. And maybe someone gave his description to the police and then identified him from a sketch. More likely, they just shrugged the whole thing off and never bothered reporting it to anyone for fear of getting into trouble. That's what things are like in your favorite hospital.

The place smelled of disinfectant, the walls were white, the corridors wide, the doctors and nurses very intent on what they were doing. Brian Baldwin was in a private room on the third floor, sleeping. Someone had brought roses. Laura was always fond of roses, though I never knew if it was the flower or the thorns that appealed to her. Baldwin, even sleeping, had a strong and not unattractive face, with the exception of his hair, which was entirely missing. His breathing was deep but not terribly so. I hid myself and waited.

After a while, when nothing happened, I slipped outside the door and read his chart. He was, it seems, twenty-five years old and a graduate student at St. Bartholomew's College. The chart contained such gems of information as: "Weak, rapid, thready pulse." What in the world is a thready pulse? It also mentioned, among the little bit I could understand, dehydration, increased heart rate, severe anemia with several question marks after it, "HIV neg" followed by three dates, the first being last September, the most recent being last month. It also contained the notes "questionably compliant," and "2-3 day cycle."

I wondered what "questionably compliant" meant. It sounded like blaming the victim for the failure of the treatment, but I don't know hospital jargon.

The most interesting one, however, was from late

last September, where it said several things about "chemo," followed by indecipherable codes, and ending with, "Leukemia negative, discontinuing chemo."

Now, I don't know a great deal about chemotherapy, but I think I have a better idea of why so much of Kellem's hair is gone—they looked at his symptoms and decided he had leukemia, and treated it with chemotherapy, and Kellem got to share in the side effects. Didn't she know it would happen? Or didn't she care? Could she really be in love?

Poor Laura.

And, while we're at it, poor doctors; they haven't a clue. Or, rather, they have every clue, but there is no chance they'll believe them.

I waited for several hours more, hiding from the nurses and watching, but nothing happened. I wasn't surprised; if he'd been my victim, I'd have waited another day or two until he recovered. And besides, why should she come so late? If I were here, I'd arrive in the early evening, like any other visitor after work. I'd probably pretend to be visiting someone else entirely, on a different floor, so that no one would connect me with the patient's relapses, and I would take advantage of the private room for a tête-à-tête with my lover, or victim, or what-have-you.

I smelled the roses once, then left via the window and came back home and put my piece of petrified wood back on, because I'm used to it. I wish those damned cops hadn't spotted it.

I do not yet know how, but I am going to kill Laura Kellem.

When I was young, I used to travel around the public houses in the evening with a friend named Robert or Richard or something. One evening I happened to finish off a glass of ale into which he had, I think by accident though I could be wrong, dropped some ash from his cigar. I can still remember spitting it out, and how disgusted I felt. That is how I feel now, although I am using the allusion to taste more in a metaphorical than a literal sense. Still, one could look at it either way, I suppose.

My hands are still shaking, and, as I typed the above paragraph, I have twice had to leave three times now I have had to run to the toilet.

But let me describe it all; perhaps that will exorcise it somewhat. I returned to the hospital and hid myself in the bathroom in Brian Baldwin's private room. Sure enough, Kellem arrived within minutes. He was awake, and they spoke together in tones too low for me to hear most of the words. But I'm certain that I heard Kellem say, "Little one."

She used to call me "Little one."

No, I'm not jealous (this time); but I understood things better now. Baldwin wouldn't or couldn't leave town, Kellem was unwilling to make him, and the bitch had fallen in love. As new for her, I think, as for me—which is hardly coincidence. So, I guess, I have something to thank her for as well.

I've been shying away from asking myself this, but I wonder if my feelings for Susan will change once I am free of Laura. I can't help wondering, but I don't believe they will. If one can ever trust one's own instincts, there is no chance that I am wrong about this.

But let me return to the story.

I continued listening, and presently the conversation stopped. I waited for a moment, then emerged from hiding. They were holding each other close, and his head was thrown back with an expression of rapture while her head was buried against his shoulder.

She looked up as I entered, and her expression underwent a series of changes impossible to describe. At last she said, "What are you doing here? How did you find me?"

Brian sighed and settled back against his pillow, calling her name softly; his breathing was fast and deep. Kellem rose from the bed and faced me.

I said, "I thought we should have a talk, dearest Laura. Have you a few moments? I hate to interrupt such a tender scene, but—"

"Keep still."

"Your hair seems to be starting to grow back. Congratu—"

"Silence."

"Heh. Try it on someone else; I know better now."

"You know what better, fool?"

"Many things. I know why you brought me here. I know what sort of idiocy you've been involved in. I know that you lied to me. Most important, I know *why* you lied to me. You cannot control me any longer, Kellem."

"Oh?" she said. "I cannot?"

"That is correct."

She smirked at me.

I shrugged. "I'm offering you a deal, Kellem. My life for yours. You leave me in peace, and allow me to depart, and I'll take no action against you."

"Indeed?" she said, smiling with fake sweetness. "But if I cannot control you, how can I stop you from leaving? Why don't you just do it?"

"It isn't quite that simple," I said. "But I can—"

"Silence," she repeated, snapping out the word, and I found myself unable to speak; it was as if something had reached past my consciousness to wherever my motor skills are controlled, and pushed the off button for speech. All I could do was glare, which I did.

"You think you can defy me? You think you can resist my will? You think you can set your powers against mine?"

I still could not speak, so I continued to glare; flying in the face of reason, I must admit, but I wasn't feeling reasonable.

"Then I must teach you better."

She looked around, and I saw her eyes come to rest on the tray of half-eaten food on the cart next to Brian's bed. I suddenly knew what she was going to do, and I tried to ask her not to but I still couldn't speak. She pointed to it and said, "Eat."

I shook my head.

"Eat," she said again, and I couldn't even fight it. I walked over to the tray, and picked up the spoon. There was some sort of noodle dish with hamburger and tomato sauce. I don't even think I would have been able to eat such a thing when

Four times now. I hope that was the last.

I picked up a spoon and put a little on it. "More," she said. I complied. I brought it to my mouth and stopped. "Do it," she said.

I did. I chewed it. I would have chewed it for a long, long time, but she caught me and said "Swallow," so I did. I felt it slide down my throat and travel all the way into my stomach.

She said, "Again."

Her control over my voice had stopped, so I said, "Laura, please—"

"Another one! Now!"

I repeated the process. And again. It was about then that the cramps hit and I doubled over, retching.

"Again," said Laura, at which point the door opened. The cramp ended as this occurred, so I was able to watch as a nurse entered. She stared at me, then gave me a disapproving frown.

"The food," she said, "is for—"

"Kill her," said Laura Kellem, and I could feel her smile as she pronounced the words.

I had no will, no choice.

The nurse screamed and backed out of the door. I was on her before she got much farther, but that was enough. I was aware that there were many people around me as my hands fastened on her throat, crushed, and twisted. At the same moment, I felt that I was free again, but it was just exactly too late.

I was back in the room before the nurse's body hit the ground. I was not surprised to find that Kellem was nowhere to be seen. Another cramp hit just as the screams started, giving me the absurd impression that everyone in the hospital had been hit with stomach cramps at the same time I was.

There were footsteps behind me, but I couldn't move. There were hands on my shoulders as the pain stopped. I stood and twisted free. Someone tried to grab me and I tossed him or her away like an insect one finds crawling on one's shirt. I crashed through the window, taking cuts on my face and hands.

I made it back home in time for my stomach to empty itself. Five times, so far.

Somehow I am going to kill Laura Kellem.

Today I went on what can only be called a scavenger hunt. I had to start early so I could reach places before they closed, but I made it. I purchased one black candle, some dark blue wool and matching thread, a needle, ten yards of blue yarn, one yard of white. Then I found an all-night grocery store and picked up some fresh basil.

So much for the purchases. The other stuff was harder, it still being winter, but I took a shaving from the stem of a wild rose, and bits of some mountain ash and even a few nettles, although it took me nearly all night and I came back cold and irritated.

When I returned, Jim said, "What's in the bag?"

"I'm going to sacrifice a child," I snapped. "Gotta problem with that?"

He looked troubled until he realized that I was jesting, which hurt my feelings a little.

For all that it has taken me, maybe ten minutes to write this down, getting it done was very lengthy and irritating. But at least I'm done, and as ready as I'm likely to be.

The moon will be new in five days.

Winter is holding on with great determination this year, which annoys me even though I know what is causing it. In New York, spring is meaningless as far as I'm concerned, and in many places I have been it never actually seems to happen, but Ohio, I'm told, usually has one, and this year we are being cheated out of it. It snowed again today, then the snow turned to rain which froze on the sidewalks after making a halfhearted effort at melting some of the snow it had just deposited on us. It had stopped raining by the time I arrived at Susan's door. The smells of spring, which are how I identify the condition, have not yet occurred, and for all I can tell will not at all this year.

We walked to the Tunnel and strolled along the Ave; one of a number of couples fighting the weather, hand in hand or arms about each other. Susan had her black-gloved hands on my arm; I had eschewed my ugly coat entirely, but wore a thick gray sweater. There is something about this particular pose—her hands on my arm—that makes me feel tall, proud, masculine, and extraordinarily tender.

I felt oddly akin to the other couples on the street, as if we were all part of an elite—the young and in love, to coin a hackneyed phrase. Most of us, I think, knew that somewhere along the line most of us would join the young and miserable, followed by the young and resigned, followed by the middle-aged and bored; but ought that to diminish the pleasure of the moment? *Au contraire,* if I may.

I said, "How is Jill?"

"She seems to be doing very well. She was up all day today, and didn't seem nearly so pale. In fact, she went out a couple of hours ago."

"Good. I will speak to her."

"You might want to wait a day or two."

"Perhaps. How did things go with Jennifer?"

"What a bitch."

I chuckled. "Is that all there is to say about it?"

"Pretty much."

I shrugged. "If you were to suddenly leave me for someone else, I'd be a bitch too." What is it that makes us want to defend our late rival? I suppose the fear that we may be in need of such defense sooner than we would like.

Susan, however, brushed off my comment and said, "Would you start listing all the things you'd done for me, as if I'm supposed to stay with you out of gratitude?"

I shook my head. "No, I'd simply find the other person and dismember him, or her."

She laughed, thinking I was joking. Or maybe not.

A couple of birds were complaining about the weather. The rats played in the sewers, the cars played on the streets. I turned my head away when patrol cars went by, which they rarely did on the Ave.

She squeezed my arm and remarked, "I've been thinking about what you said."

"About dismemberment?"

She laughed. "About maybe coming along when and if you leave."

"Oh." One of the amazing things about Susan is her ability to talk about the most serious things without losing the laughter in her voice. I said, "What about it?"

She was quiet for a moment, then she said, "I know so little about you."

"You know that I love you; that's a start."

"Now," she said, "you're being trite."

I sighed. "I suppose I am. What do you want to know?"

"Well, what do you do for a living?"

"Many things. I play cards, for one."

"Gamble?"

Déjà vu. "No gamble," I said, and smiled.

She laughed. "What else do you do?"

"Pretty young girls."

She laughed again. I love her laugh. It somehow manages to be simultaneously contrived and natural. She said, "All right, then where do you live?"

"With a friend, a few miles from here."

"What's it like?"

"Do you wish to see it?"

"Yes."

"Now?"

She shrugged. "There's no hurry."

"All right. Tomorrow, then."

"That would be splendid."

"What else do you want to know?"

"Everything about you. Where were you born?"

"Far away across the sundering sea. I was educated in London, though, and that probably has more of an effect on me than my birthplace."

"You seem to have lost most of the accent, although I like what's left."

"Thank you. What else do you want to know?"

"My, we *are* in an expansive mood today, aren't we?"

"Anything your heart desires, my love; today it shall be yours."

"Well, in that case."

"Yes?"
"Let's go back to my house."
And we did.
F.D.S.N.

The deed is done, the bird has flown.

Or something like that.

And I had never suspected what sort of bird it was; I'm not certain I know now, only—

But let me tell it as it happened.

I awoke, and decided that it was time to finish things with Jill. I admit I thought seriously of killing her, but it was too likely to cause complications, and it was really only a matter of convenience and saving myself some annoyance, which made it a poor risk.

I brought her to mind, and was startled at once; I recognized where she was and what she was doing.

Well, one place was as good as another. It took me half an hour to walk there, and that was because I strolled; keeping an eye out for the police, but also because of the weather, which had become colder, and kept the sidewalks treacherous. The stars were out, blazing, and the moon had not yet risen, nor would it until nearly dawn.

I'm certain that Jill did not hear me approach her, yet when I got there she was sitting on a tall stool, waiting for me. She wore a dark blue smock over whatever else she had on. The blue was, in fact, only theoretical; the smock was covered with paint splatters and would probably have been stylish, somewhere. There was another stool, a few feet from hers, so I sat on it, and looked at the easel.

It glistened with fresh acrylic. At first I thought it was a still life. There were a bunch of white roses against a pale red background, and something about these roses made me understand why some cultures consider white to be a sign of mourning, because, although the roses were in full bloom, very beautiful and lifelike, there was a quality of death about them; perhaps in the way they lay in the clear vase; a haphazard arrangement as if someone had picked them and then thrown them into the vase, not caring how they looked. Rather than admiring their beauty, it made me speculate on picking roses at all; on what one did when one took a blooming flower and cut it from the bush.

And then I noticed that behind the vase, almost invisible, in some sort of impossible red on red, was a face, staring out at the viewer, as if to watch him watch the roses, and while I couldn't really see the features of that face, I knew it was a girl, and I knew that there was a single tear running down her face.

For quite a while I couldn't speak, only stare, and wonder at the choking in my throat. I finally said, "What do you call it?"

" 'Self-portrait With Roses,' " she said.

"A good name."

"Yes."

I looked some more, letting the catharsis wash over me, and when it had, I realized that it was as much a portrait of me as it was of her, and that it was not flattering.

I said, in a voice barely above a whisper, "Jill, this is magnificent."

"Thank you," she said; her voice was neither loud nor soft, but, rather, inanimate, maybe even numb.

"I had no idea you could paint like that."

"I couldn't, before," she said. "I suppose I ought to thank you."

I looked at her looking at me, and I shook my head, unable to speak. I turned back to the painting, and in this mirror I was reflected; for me to see, and all the world. I don't understand all that I felt then, but there was grief, and there was shame.

I said, "Come to me."

She got up and stood before me, letting her smock fall to the ground. She wore a dark plaid workshirt, and as she reached for the top button I said, "No."

She looked faintly puzzled, but stopped.

I took her hands in mine. "Look at me," I said.

She did.

I squeezed her hands, willing myself into her mind, her heart, her soul. Her eyes grew larger, and in them, too, I could see my own reflection, for there is no silver there, nor, for that matter, is there any gold; perhaps there is only the gentle, soft fibers of a rose.

I said, "Jill Quarrier, you are free of me. Your life is your own."

I felt her tremble through her hands, which seemed as cold as my own.

"Never again will I come to you, never again must you come to me. Your destiny is in your own hands, to make, or to destroy. You are part of me no longer, nor am I part of you. Go your way in peace."

I let go of her hands and she fell to her knees, sobbing. I bent down and kissed the top of her head, and left her that way.

I don't know.

Had she not painted that picture, I would have freed her anyway, for I had promised two people that I would, and I had already decided to keep this promise; but I wonder: If I had not, would I have released her anyway, after seeing what she could do, who she was?

In truth, I fear that I would not have, for my needs are strong and my patterns are ingrained very deeply.

But I am glad that it happened as it did, for I think it is indecent for anyone to go through his entire life and never know shame.

FIFTEEN

res·pite *n.* 1. A temporary cessation or postponement, usually of something disagreeable; an interval of rest or relief. 2. *Law.* The temporary suspension of a death sentence; a reprieve.

AMERICAN HERITAGE DICTIONARY

After setting down what had happened between Jill and me, I took myself up to the attic and pawed through the leftover books. It struck me, as it hadn't before, to wonder why they had been left behind. I can believe someone like Carpenter might, leaving in a hurry, have abandoned an old typewriting machine, and a few pieces of third-rate furniture, but these books are probably valuable; I can only assume he didn't know they were up here.

It made me wonder what else was in the attic, so I spent some time looking around. The attic is quite spacious, and mostly empty, but I found an old coffee maker; a set of silver that was probably worth something; a set of knives, stuck carelessly into a cardboard box, that included a very nice chef's knife with part of the handle stripped away; a box full of canceled checks; and a peculiar sign, which consisted of a red "R" with a circle and an arrow growing from it, and the words "Pickup Wednesdays" inscribed in red letters.

Attached to it was a pointed stick, presumably for putting it into the ground. I held it for a moment, and I thought of Laura Kellem. But come, let's be serious; wood like that would splinter and, in any case, the wood is strictly symbolic; if her heart is destroyed, that will be that. I set the sign down again.

On the other hand, it forced me to think seriously about killing her, which brought to mind the ritual I will be attempting at the dark of the moon, in two days' time. Do I really think I can kill her? Will I if I get the chance?

Laura Kellem is a vindictive soul; it may be that she feels she has not punished me enough. And if she does, indeed, feel that way, than not only am I in danger, but so is Susan.

I tested the edge of the chef's knife, found a butcher's steel in the box and honed the knife. It had been a long, long time since I'd done that, but I managed not to cut myself.

I brought the knife down from the attic with me, and it is sitting beside me now, looking out of place on top of the pile of paper that records my visit to Lakota. When I have finished typing this, I shall take the knife with me as I go to rest, and I will place it with the rest of the items I have assembled for the ritual.

Two days.

Two days out of a lifetime of, well, of many thousands of days, and yet it seems impossibly far off.

Little to talk about tonight, but I must feed my addiction to this machine. I sneaked out of the house, past the watching policemen, and came to Susan's, where I found an envelope with my name on it taped to her door. The note inside said, "Jonathan, sorry, forgot I have a dance ensemble tonight. See you tomorrow? Take me to your house? Maybe we can spend the night. Love, Susan."

Her name was signed with a big scrawl coming from the *n* and underlining her name. I mentally shrugged.

I walked around the campus area for a while, then spent an hour or so in Little Philly, not doing anything, just watching the people go by. There are so many of them: Decrepit old bums to well-to-do young white couples, the pimps, the whores, the crack dealers, and gangs of black kids filled with the delicious pleasure of knowing that you are intimidating anyone who walks past, just by existing.

I walked all the way back to the Tunnel, which took a couple of hours, and I visited some of the places that Susan and I had been to. With any luck, I'll be leaving this city in two days, so this was a sort of farewell. Some snow had melted, although the wind still had its bite. Winter doesn't want to give up, but it is a losing battle.

The contrast between the Tunnel and Little Philly, which are really the only areas of Lakota I've come to know at all, is so sharp that it is hard to believe that they are part of the same city; but I like them both, and the presence of each makes the other that much richer. It's funny, but I've never been downtown, or to the Longfellow Park district, or by the Lakeshore; entire areas, like cities within the city, and I don't know what they are like. For that matter, there are parts of London I know nothing about, and I spent many years there. Maybe it is time to go back and do some serious exploring.

Another odd thing is that now I think I understand Laura better than I did when we had that talk, so many months ago. I think she was telling the truth when we first spoke: This would be a nice place to live, to settle down.

There is little that I have ever done that I actually regret, but, do you know, I'm sorry about that dog, Pepper. And I'm glad I didn't give in to my instincts when I wanted to kill Bill's wife. I hope all of this doesn't

sour them on the neighborhood; it will be a good place
again, once I have broken free of Kellem and left.

The night grows old, the day approaches, and, as
always, I run.

It has been an entire day since I have seen Susan.

My lover is sleeping on the bloodstained gray chair
downstairs.

The house was cold and dry as I made my way up to
the bathroom earlier this evening, from which I con-
cluded that the dogs of winter still held the weather and
would shake it with at least a few more days of cold
before dropping it and retreating once more to await
November.

When I came back down, feeling strangely at peace
after a dreamless sleep, Jim was still standing by the
window. "Still there," he said.

It took me a moment to realize that he meant the
police, then I said, "It doesn't matter."

For maybe the second or third time since I've known
him he looked right at me. "What happened?" he said.

I shrugged. "A bit of a surprise, is all. People sometimes turn out to be, I don't know, not what I'd thought
they'd be."

"Is that good or bad?"

"Good, but also upsetting. I begin to think I make
too many hasty judgments."

He nodded and went back to looking out the window while I got my coat on. He said nothing else as I left
the house. I went carefully, making certain I wasn't spotted. Outside, the last traces of purple-red sunset were
absorbed by the soft glow of the lights of Mark Twain
College, a couple of miles to the west. The wind was light
but steady; I kept my hands in the pocket of my parka.
There were a few slippery spots where snow had melted
and then frozen again, but they weren't too bad.

I knocked at the door and Susan answered. I was glad it wasn't Jill because I really didn't know what I'd find to say to her, what with one thing and another. I hung up my coat, took off my Wellingtons, kissed Susan, and said, "So, what do you want to do?"

She grinned, spun once, then gyrated her pelvis lewdly.

"I meant after that," I said.

"After that? Hmmm. Perhaps you could take me to Baghdad. I've always wanted to see Baghdad."

"During a war?"

"The war's over. But you're right. Maybe somewhere else."

"We'll talk about it," I said, and held out my arm. She curtsied, dimpled, laid her hand on top of mine, and we ascended into heaven, as it were.

I was very careful with her, and gentle, trying to give as much as I could while taking as little as possible. I must have been successful, because she seemed quite pleased, and did not fall asleep.

We spoke of school, and her hopes for the future, and her love of dancing, and the exhilaration of being before an audience; a pleasure I've never felt, but can almost understand. She asked about me and I avoided answering. I asked about her and she told me some things. She talked about grabbing what she could from life; I talked about waiting while life delivered whatever I wanted.

"I don't have the patience for that," she said.

"You want it now."

"Instant gratification," she agreed. "I hate waiting."

"I will remember that."

"I told you about the bus."

"That's true; I'd forgotten. When that happens, it's time to get a car."

"I hate cars," she said.

"If truth be known, so do I. But I hate buses, too."

"What do you like?" she said.

"Walking."

"How do you feel about flying."

"Flying is okay; depends on how one does it."

"Ships?"

"Only when necessary," I said.

She shook her head. "I like to travel."

"I like to be other places; I don't like getting there."

"We can work it out," she said.

"I would imagine we can."

Then she said, "So, would you like to show me your house?"

"Now?"

"Why not? Is it cold?"

"Not horribly."

"Well then?"

"All right; let's go."

She put on a dark blue skirt and a Twain sweatshirt, brushed her hair, stuck a blue band in it, kissed me, and pronounced herself ready.

As I type this, the problem with bringing her to my home is staring at me so hard that I can't believe I didn't notice it at the time; I guess my head was so filled with Susan that there was no room for anything else. We walked through the Tunnel, arm in arm, talking about alternate energy sources, oil wars, and yellow journalism, and as we turned onto Twenty-eighth it suddenly hit me, and I stopped dead; I believe I felt perspiration on my forehead in spite of the cold, but my imagination may have supplied that later.

"What is it?" she said.

I stood there, unable to answer. It is one thing to know that I can circumvent the police, quite another to expect Susan to do so; particularly when she didn't even know they were there.

So, what to do?

I stood there for what seemed like forever, trying to think of a way out of this, while Susan said, "Jonathan? What is it? Are you all right?" I could change my mind about showing her the house. I played that conversation over in my mind and decided against it. I could tell her we had to sneak in, and then explain that . . . no.

I shook my head and said, "It's nothing, love. A thought just came to me, but it doesn't matter."

When there are no easy ways, you take the hard way, right? Right.

I pulled up the hood of my parka and approached the rust brown '89 Plymouth from behind, and after telling Susan I had to ask these gentlemen something, I put my head next to the passenger door and rapped on the glass. Two men were in it, both seemed to be in their early thirties. Maybe taxi drivers turn into policemen in their middle years. They looked at me. One was dark and had a fleshy face with a high nose, the other had short, light-colored hair, blue eyes, a fair complexion, and a pointed chin.

He rolled down the window, started to ask what I wanted, then turned his head quickly to glance at the sketch on the clipboard on the seat between them.

That was as far as he got before he fell asleep. His partner actually reached into his coat before slumping forward against the steering wheel, and my knees were shaking.

When I turned around, Susan was standing right behind me, staring at them. "What happened? Should we call an ambulance?"

I looked her in the eye. "Nothing happened."

"But—"

"Nothing happened. We just walked by this car, not even stopping, and we never looked through the window. Nothing happened."

"Nothing happened," she repeated dully.

We took two steps toward the house and I said, "Snap out of it, Susan."

"Huh, what?"

"You were daydreaming."

"Oh. Hmmm. Maybe I'm short on sleep."

"Could be. You can sleep at the house, if you want to."

"How much farther is it?"

"We're here."

"This place?"

"Is something wrong?"

"No, it's *beautiful.* When was it built?"

"I don't know. Late nineteenth century, I think."

She looked at it, studying as well as she could in the relative dark; the nearest streetlight is half a block away. She said, "I'd like to see it in the daylight. How far around does the porch go?"

"About halfway."

"Is that window stained—hey, you haven't shoveled the walk."

"Sorry."

"No, I mean, why aren't there any tracks?"

"I usually leave by the back door, but I wanted you to see the front."

"Oh. Why is there orange tape across the door?"

"Don't ask. Go under it."

I tried the knob and said, "That's right. It's locked. Wait here and I'll let you in. Shan't be a minute."

" 'Crime Site'?" she read from the tape.

"Don't ask," I repeated.

"All right."

I slipped inside, turned on the one working light in the living room, and let her in. She stepped into the entryway and said, "Jonathan, this is splendid."

"Thanks. Rent-free, too."

"It is?" She stared.

"Well, officially no one lives here."

"You mean you—"

"Right."

"Why?"

I shrugged. "Easier this way."

"Who owns it?"

"A professor at Twain. Carpenter."

"French Lit?"

"Right."

"Does he know you're living here?"

"I keep forgetting to look him up and tell him."

She shook her head, puzzled, I guess, and looked at the woodwork that was there, the woodwork that had been removed, the stained glass, the floors, the high ceilings. She looked back at me to say something, then frowned. "Jonathan, are you all right?"

"Why do you ask?"

"I don't know; you look ill."

"I'm feeling a little shaky, but it's all right."

"Are you certain?"

I nodded. About then, Jim came down the stairs, noticed the light, and said, "Won't the police notice if you leave that on in here?"

I shook my head.

Susan said, "That's funny."

"What?"

"I don't know. I thought for a minute . . . Jonathan, is this place haunted?"

"Not unpleasantly so. I didn't know you believed in ghosts."

"I'm not sure that I do," she said. "But . . ." Her voice trailed off into silence.

"Come on, let's look at the rest of the house."

"Yes, let's."

I showed her the rest of the house. She made several

comments to the effect that it didn't look lived in, and several more about the fixtures (she seemed especially delighted that the old gas lamps were still in place, even though there was no gas coming through the pipes), but most of her discussion was about how she would fix it up. She spoke of Victorian-style furnishings without the Victorian love of clutter; of the painting that would go above the fireplace, of William Morris wallpaper.

She was enchanted with the kitchen, and spoke of cooking some crepes. I smiled noncommittally and mumbled something. She said, "You don't have a refrigerator."

"No, but isn't the stove clean?"

"You don't cook much, do you?"

"I must admit I've never really learned how."

"I'll teach you," she said. "But you'll have to get a refrigerator."

She tsked at the shape the basement was in, and spoke of finishing it, while I went over in my mind some of the practical considerations of the two of us traveling together. Funny I hadn't thought of any of this before. *What's in the trunk, dear? Oh, nothing important.* And, *Where are you going, darling? Oh, I'll be gone again until this evening.* Looked at that way, the whole thing was absurd.

The answer was simple enough. All I had to do was tell her—let her know. Hand her a silvered mirror and say, "What's wrong with this picture?"

I wasn't certain I could do it.

I discovered that I was trembling slightly, and decided that my mood and my thoughts were probably the aftereffects of my condition; dealing with the cops had, as Susan noticed, left me pretty shaken. But there was no good way to solve that just then. I knew I was going to have to before tomorrow midnight, when I intended to perform the ritual to break myself from Kellem, but I had time.

When I showed her the upstairs, she lit on the type-writing machine at once, saying, "Good heavens. Does it work?"

"Yes, I've been using it."

"For what?"

"For writing love poems to you."

She smiled, her eyes very wide. "Not really."

I shrugged with my eyebrows and smiled back with my lips.

She said, "May I see them?"

"Maybe. Let me work up the courage, first."

I showed her the rest of the upstairs. She loved the L-shaped master bedroom and library combination, with its own fireplace, and asked why I didn't have my bed in there. I said, "I can't sleep far off the ground."

She said, "Where do you sleep?"

"In the basement."

"Really? Isn't it uncomfortable?"

"Not terribly. I'll show you later."

"All right. What's this?"

"Linen closet."

"Oh. Why is it empty?"

"Why keep things up here when I sleep in the base-ment?"

"That makes sense. You must kiss me now."

"All right, there."

"You must always kiss me when we pass the linen closet; it's an old Roman custom I just invented."

"And a good one."

"Why is that wall shaped so funny?"

"The chimney is behind it."

"But the fireplace is on the other side."

"The master-bedroom fireplace is, this is the chim-ney from downstairs."

"Two chimneys?"

"Well, either they didn't know how to connect two fireplaces to one chimney, or they just felt like having fireplaces on different sides of the house."

"Conspicuous consumption."

"Yes."

"It's grand."

"Here's the bathroom. It works, and there's even toilet paper."

"Good. Excuse me for a moment."

Left to myself, I discovered that I had worked up the courage. I found my stack of manuscript and pulled out ten or eleven of the poems I'd written. I left two in the stack; one that I didn't like much and another that I didn't want her to see because, well, I don't know. I had the pile of papers hidden again before she came out.

I handed the pages to her, and she said, "All of this? You wrote these for me?" She seemed inordinately pleased; it was almost embarrassing. "Can I read them now?"

"All right. The only comfortable chair is in the living room. I'm afraid it's stained, but it shouldn't come off."

"All right."

She went tripping down the stairs, my poems in her hand. I stayed in the typing room and took several deep breaths. While I was doing so, Jim came into the room.

I said, "Do you mind the company?"

"Not at all," he said. "But I'm worried about the police."

"Don't. The two down the block are sleeping."

He looked uncomfortable. "Are you sure there aren't any more?"

"Well, no. I hope not."

"Me, too. And what will happen when someone comes to investigate why they haven't called in?"

"I'll go turn the light off."

"Yes," he said.

I went down, and found that Susan was sitting in the chair, my poems in her lap, and there were tears on her cheeks. I stood over her and kissed her forehead.

She looked at me, her eyes so bright and shimmering with tears, and held up the pages as if she wanted to say something, then set them down, shaking her head slowly. If this is all the critical acclaim I ever get, it is enough. "Sleep now, my love," I said.

She nodded. I turned off the light, then came back to the typewriting machine. Jim wasn't in the room, so I have taken the opportunity to set it all down. I'm not certain what to do now. I cannot risk taking Susan out of here, so perhaps it would be best if she slept with me, which, after all, she did ask about once. I will keep her sleeping, because I feel no need to shock her in that way, but it will be pleasant to rest with her in my arms, though she knows it not. Perhaps she will dream of it, and we will share the joy that way.

SIXTEEN

in·no·cent *adj.* 1. Uncorrupted by evil, malice, or wrong-doing; sinless; untainted; pure: *as innocent of evil as a child.* 2.a. Not guilty of a specific crime; legally blame-less: *found innocent of all charges.* b. Not responsible for or guilty of something wrong or unethical; not to be accused: *innocent of negligence . . . n.* 1. A person who is free or relatively free of evil or sin; one who is pure or uncorrupted. 2. A simple, guileless, inex-perienced, or unsophisticated person; one who is vul-nerable or credulous.

AMERICAN HERITAGE DICTIONARY

The new moon, as I look out through the slats, is a spot of darkness near the western horizon, and only barely visible even to me. Susan sleeps once more. There is no reason for her to be awake.

Yesterday, while she slept deeply, I carried her downstairs and took her with me while I rested. I had never done that—actually slept with a lover in my arms, and I felt such a tenderness that I thought my heart would break.

We slept undisturbed, and I had no dreams, al-though perhaps Susan did. We began to wake at almost the same moment. Her eyes fluttered open and she looked into my own. Confusion came over her brow, so I smoothed it by kissing her.

"Where are we?" she said.

"In my bed."

"But it is so dark. It feels—"

"Hush, my love."

I kissed her again. The kiss became intense, and at last weakness and urgency conspired against me. She moaned softly and held me close, and it came to me that I was killing her.

I stopped abruptly and looked at her; she was very pale, and seemed to have some trouble breathing. I cursed myself silently, rose, brought her up to the parlor, and set her in the chair. She appeared to be very pale, her breath was coming in ragged gasps.

I am glad I did not kill her; sorry I came so close.

Still, it gave me what I needed; I feel ready for whatever midnight will bring.

Jim was standing next to the chair, watching me. He made no comment.

I said, "Any more police?"

"No."

"Good."

"Are you going to do it?"

"Break away from Kellem? Yes. In just about three hours."

"Do you think it will work?"

"I hope so."

I returned to my typewriting sanctuary to try to finish memorizing the procedure, which I will be about as soon as I am done

Kellem is either one step ahead of me, or one step behind; soon I will learn which it is. As I was typing merrily away, there were police pulling up outside the house. Jim came and informed me of this.

I slipped outside to see for myself. The police are everywhere. I saw neighbors peering through windows down the street, and others, including Bill and his wife, standing staring at my house.

And there was a van that bore the inscription "WBBM Mobile News." Apparently the news people still aren't certain of anything, because, as I watched, the van drove away.

It was tricky, getting close enough to hear what the police were up to, but I did, and I don't like what I learned. They are waiting for something they called the "Tac Group," which sounds ominous. And eventually I learned why they are there, and what they are going to do.

Someone told them that, hidden in this very house, lived the man who had killed a certain Philip Hansen. It took me a bit longer to learn that Philip Hansen had been the night editor for the *Plainsman*.

I have a guess who told them, too.

Laura Kellem, damn you to hell.

The worst of it is that they saw the light on in the typing room, and, as I understand it, someone even got a glimpse of me in the living room, using some sort of modern binoculars, so they know I'm here. Certainly I can slip past them as often as I want, but Susan cannot; and neither can I bring my luggage with me. Traveling without it will be inconvenient at best. I've had to do such things before, and I didn't like it.

I must consider how to get Susan out of here. Hiding in my alcove is all well and good, but if they know I am somewhere in the house, and they search thoroughly, they could certainly find her.

The easiest thing, I guess, will be to explain the situation to her, and have her convince the police that I was holding her against her will. They will still wonder how I could have gotten past them, but that is hardly my problem. Let them wonder.

I am not looking forward to explaining this to Susan.

I found the cop in charge, a fat man with graying hair who I'd have thought was too short to be a policeman. He and his cohorts were trying to decide if they should go in when the "Tac Group" arrived, or wait until morning, when there was less chance of "a negative incident," which I took to mean a neighbor getting shot. They spoke of evacuating the nearby houses.

I exerted a little influence, and I think they will wait until morning, by which time I will be gone.

Morning, however, is still many hours away; and the time until midnight is growing short. I must not allow myself to be distracted. First, I will break free of Kellem, then worry about the next step.

I have gathered together everything I will need, including the chef's knife; now I have little to do except record what has happened and wait for midnight.

I still have over an hour to wait, and the time is passing with agonizing slowness. Every few minutes I stop and pick up this paper on which I have scrawled the steps of the spell I am to perform, so that, when the time comes, I will have it firmly in mind, and so that I need not stop to read, but can proceed smoothly from memory. The old woman said that would help.

After all of this, it would be the ultimate irony if I have allowed myself to be fooled by the *cigány*—if the instructions on this paper are meaningless.

Yet, I think they are not. There is Jill's example, and what I read corresponds to what I remember.

Speculation is pointless. Soon I will know.

I have run out of things to say; the time for action approaches.

I went down once more to check on all of the items for the ritual and to stretch my legs. Jim was there, looking out the window. He said, "They might try to come in."

"Not likely," I said.

"Oh?"

"Trust me."

He nodded.

Susan was looking maybe a little better. She stirred as I watched her and called my name. I shivered, though I cannot name the emotion that evoked the shiver.

I knelt beside her and said, "I am here, my love."

Her eyes opened and she smiled, weakly. "I don't feel—I have had the oddest dreams, Jonathan." Her voice was very soft, and though she was breathing easier than she had earlier, it still seemed to take some effort.

Still kneeling, I took her hand. It was not as warm as it usually is, and I silently cursed myself for bringing her to this state.

"It's the house, my love. It brings bad dreams."

She nodded and brought my hand to her cheek. Then she squinted, staring over my shoulder, and said, "Who is that?"

I followed the direction of her gaze and said, "That is Jim, a friend of mine."

"Oh. Hello, Jim."

"Hello, Susan," he said.

She studied him a little more, then frowned and closed her eyes. "Am I awake?" she said.

"I don't know," I told her. "Would you like to be?"

"I'm not certain. I feel like I'm dreaming."

"Then perhaps you are."

"Do you love me in my dream?"

"In your dream, in my dream, and when we are awake, I love you the same."

She smiled and pressed my hand once more to her cheek. "Then it doesn't matter." She leaned her head back to rest it against the back of the chair, and breathed deeply. I thought she had gone to sleep again, but she opened her eyes and said, "When you leave, I'd like to come with you."

"I would like that, too," I said.

"I've been having such odd dreams, Jonathan."

"Tell me about them."

"I dreamt that you were dead, and that I was dead, only we both lived."

"Interesting." I almost told her then, but I think it will be better to wait until she is at least a little stronger.

She said, "I dreamt that I was dancing for all eternity, and that the more I danced, the more I lived, and the more I lived, the more I wanted to dance." She grinned weakly. "Dancing is my life, or something."

"Would you like to live forever, to dance forever?"

She smiled complacently. "If you were there."

"I will always be there."

"Then I will dance," she said, and, with a sigh, she relaxed against the chair. Her breathing slowed a little, and presently she was asleep again. I watched for a moment, then placed her hand in her lap and came back upstairs, almost choking with emotion. Jim, bless his heart, didn't say anything.

It is almost time. I will go over the steps of the rite once or twice again. I only have another half hour or so to chew my figurative nails. And then . . .

SEVENTEEN

save[1] *v.—tr.* 1. To rescue from harm, danger, or loss; bring to a safe condition. 2. To keep in a safe, intact condition; safeguard. 3. To prevent or reduce the waste, loss, or expenditure of. 4. To keep for future use or enjoyment; store. Often used with *up*. 5. To treat with care in order to avoid fatigue, wear, or damage; to spare. 6. To make unnecessary, obviate: *This will save you an extra trip.* 7. *Theology.* To deliver from sin or the wages of sin; redeem.

AMERICAN HERITAGE DICTIONARY

Words, as they appear on a piece of typing paper, are flat and lifeless when compared to the sound of a voice, or even words written with a good pen. The only expression of emotion, beyond the words themselves, is in the variation of darkness or lightness of each letter, which might give a clue to the state of mind of the writer. One sees the words, but does not know if they flowed effortlessly from the fingers, or if each was the product of wracking consideration; one has no way of telling, from the evidence before him, that perhaps the writer's hands twitched back and forth a few times, hesitant, tentative, intimidated by the unmarked paper before him and the weight of experiences behind him.

Jim keeps coming in, looking at me, saying a few words, and leaving. He did so twice before I started typing, and once since I set down the paragraph engraved above. I have the impression he is worried about me. It is a good feeling to know that someone worries about you. I worry about Susan, but, as I type, she is safe in another room behind thick walls.

Let us put everything in order, as if the cold, evenly spaced letters were reflections of a calm, well-ordered mind, unmoved by turmoil within or distractions without, and I will note in passing that, were the walls of this house less thick, I might not be able to write at all. And from this, I am given to wonder if it matters, but leave that.

Let me return my thoughts to midnight, an eternity and a few short hours ago, when Jim and I came down to the parlor. Dust had gathered on the oak coat tree, but the maple floor still shone like new. There were a couple of sheets stuck into a corner, as if someone had used them to cover furniture and then abandoned them when the furniture was moved. The ceiling fixture hung in the center, impotent from lack of gas or bulbs.

I stood in the middle of the room and picked up the blue yarn. I held it for a moment, caressing it and wondering and thinking about what was to come. If what I was about to do was anything other than nonsense, than it was a skill, and it is the nature of skills that they improve with practice; I was trying something very difficult, and very important, as my first effort in ritual magic.

Yet, and it makes me smile ironically to consider it, that was not what nearly prevented me from beginning; nor was it the fear of the consequences from Kellem if I failed; rather it was the thought, as I contemplated the ritual whose steps I had so carefully memorized, that it was an absurd series of things to be doing and saying.

My conversation with the old woman kept coming back. "The state of your mind will be most important as you perform the ritual," she had said.

"But how can I control the state of my mind?"

"That's what the ritual is for."

"Circular reasoning," I said.

"It is not," she had said, "a reasonable matter."

I slowly laid the yarn out in a circle around myself and my tools, walking clockwise and saying, "May flames consume the evil around me, may Mother Earth shield me from evil, may the winds blow evil from me, and the oceans wash the evil away." I laid three rows of the yarn, repeating this as I went.

To be perfectly honest, it felt ridiculous, especially with Jim watching, and I kept wondering if the old woman had lied to me; at the same time, I tried to put meaning into the hollow-sounding phrases. But what is "evil"? If there is such a thing, then could it not describe me? Or is it relative and practical—with evil defined as anything the practitioner doesn't like? I didn't know and I still don't; only now I no longer care; then I must have, for such were my thoughts as I walked the fairy ring.

When it was done, I set the candle in the center, and lit it; the sound of the kitchen match igniting seemed unnaturally loud, as did the sputtering of the wax when the wick caught. The fire danced and flickered, making shadows on the walls—shadows of the coat tree and of the ceiling fixture, from which false crystals hung, throwing shades like a thousand little knives. For just a moment, I thought I saw Jim's shadow, wavering in and out of existence in time to the dance of the flame, but perhaps not. I sat down on the floor, facing south.

I picked up needle, thread, and cloth, and began work on the poppet; I found it rather easier to make than I'd expected. I discovered that I ought to have purchased a thimble, but its lack was only an annoyance. And, as I sewed, I thought about Laura Kellem—everything she had done to me and for me, the things we had shared, the hatreds I had accrued. I had no hairs from her head, nor parings of her fingernails, as the recipe called for, but I had a piece of the mountain ash, and shavings of wild rose, and a crude drawing of her that I had made on a small piece of cardboard, and I had memories, and these things went into the poppet of black silk, sewn with black thread.

It was strange work. I would think of Kellem, perhaps remembering nights spent riding through the London Underground, doing nothing but laughing and joking and watching people, and then I would be distracted by the back of the needle poking into my thumb, and then I would think of Susan, sleeping on the chair in the next room, and then I would remember the hospital room, and I would hate.

And as I worked, I began to say her name, over and over, until it became a chant; an image of her began to grow in my mind. I held it there, still chanting. My hands went through the sewing motions on their own, and I had no need to concentrate on the chant, either; my only thoughts were of Laura Kellem and the image of her that grew until it seemed almost three-dimensional, hanging in the air before my mind's eye.

After a time, the poppet was finished.

Then I stopped chanting, held it before me, looked at it, and said, "You are Laura Kellem." And I meant it. There was no longer any feeling of absurdity to my actions; the rite had taken me, and was working me as I worked it. As the *cigány* had said, that must be the purpose of ritual; it guided me into what I must feel, the way an irrigation ditch will guide water; it doesn't matter if the water doesn't take the ditch seriously, it still goes where it must.

I felt as if my actions were those of a weaver and what I was weaving was myself, all my actions, all of my being, all of my desires into a tapestry of hope and will. Yet, at the same time, there was the curious sense of being outside of it all, of standing next to myself watching as I went through these strange motions, said these strange things, and hoped for this impossible and inevitable outcome.

I set the poppet aside and picked up a piece of white thread, and three knots I made in it, and as I made the knots I said, "So I am bound. So I am bound. So I am bound." The words echoed in my head as they reverberated through the room, and who knows how much was real, and who cares?

And in black thread I wrapped the poppet, very tight, covering it all, and saying, "You cannot touch me. You cannot see me. You cannot harm me. You cannot touch me. You cannot see me. You cannot harm me. You cannot touch me. You cannot see me. You cannot harm me."

And when she was bound so that no trace of her remained uncovered I held her before me and pronounced, with terrible clarity, "You have no power over me." I wanted to believe that, and I almost did, too; I had a feeling like the twang of a plucked cello string, somewhere below the level of my awareness. But I didn't know if I heard it inside my head, in the room, or somewhere else entirely, and by this time I couldn't slow down to consider.

I cut off the end of the black thread and I tied it into three knots, and I think I said something then, too, but I can no longer remember what it was; I think a verse or two of a poem by Byron.

I set the poppet down, and I suddenly knew that Kellem was in the room, in the flesh, and she was speaking, powerfully, urgently; I felt her more than heard her, but it seemed to come from a great distance. For an instant the ritual wavered, but my hands knew what to do, even as my nerve faltered. I stuck the white thread into the candle's flame, and as the three knots burned, I felt my lips move, and I heard myself saying, "So I am free."

It was unmistakable now; the rumble of bass strings, a shiver up my spine; the feeling of a weight being suddenly lifted from my shoulders, a weight I had not, until then, known I bore. But now that I felt it, I knew, too, that it had been lightened, not removed entirely, and my determination rose with my hopes.

Far away, Kellem raged, and she fought for my attention, but I wasn't really there, or she wasn't; we were, at that time, inhabitants of different worlds.

"So I am free."

"You are not!" she cried. "You are mine!" but the knots that held me were loosening, and I smiled at the sudden feeling of release, of freedom, of victory.

"So I am free," I said.

"Mine, now and forever," she said, and I was so startled by the sudden clarity in her voice that I looked at her. She caught my eye, and she nailed me to the spot; it was like the heat when a furnace door is suddenly opened, that blast of will, and in spite of myself I flinched.

"You are mine," she repeated, and the words seemed to take life, and strike at my brain like a burrowing animal; to combat them was arduous, to ignore them, impossible. She called on me to surrender myself, and when I refused she struck at me with her rage, the twin to my own, so long ago it now seemed. We held so, energetic in our motionlessness, for a timeless time, but no matter how I fought, I felt myself slipping, as if my fingers had grasped the one rock that could keep me from the abyss, and I just wasn't strong enough.

At which point, suddenly, inexplicably, her concentration broke. I don't know how I could have missed what happened, except I was looking at Kellem as through a narrow tunnel, and everything outside was invisible or irrelevant. When her concentration broke, I had no time to wonder why, but I resumed the ritual with an urgency that seemed to come from the rite itself, rather than from me, and there is no clearer way to put it than that.

"So I am free," I said for the fourth, unnecessary time, and I wanted to laugh, for I felt that the weight was gone; I was my own man, and I knew that she could never dominate my will again. I turned my eyes from her and blew out the candle. She leapt at me, but there was something about the circle of thread; she couldn't get past it. I laughed in her face, at her rage; revenge was mine, for those few sweet seconds. I hold them even now in my mind, and perhaps there has been no greater joy in my life than savoring that eternal instant when I thought I had won fully.

Then, as I picked up the end of the blue thread and looked at her, and past her, I saw how she had been distracted: Susan was lying like a broken toy against the wall. I stood, and I stared, and I began to tremble.

She must have woken up and seen what was going on, and, in all ignorance, attacked Kellem from behind. Uselessly, in the sense that Susan could not hurt her, yet it had been exactly what I needed. How much had she known? How much had she understood? It doesn't matter.

Was she breathing? Yes, but there was also blood flowing from a wound in her throat, and she couldn't afford to lose blood. I looked back at Laura, and her hands were stained, blood dripping to the floor from her long, sharp nails.

I shook my head in denial, which turned to rage. But the ritual was not yet over, and I knew, then, how to change the program. I said, "You want to get to me, Laura? I'll help." I took up the circle, walking widdershins, very quickly, and I said, "The oceans have washed you from me, Laura; the four winds have swept you from my life; my mother, the Earth, has sheltered me; the fire is in my hand, and now—" I picked up the kitchen knife, and suddenly yanked the rest of the thread away. "And now may you burn in Hell."

She leapt at me, I suspect too full of hate to even notice that I was armed. I raised the knife, and struck, and she impaled herself on the weapon. Even as the shock traveled up my arm, I drove it into her so that it was buried almost to the hilt in her heart, and, looking into her eyes, I turned the handle a half turn, adjusting my grip, then held the knife in place, her body almost touching mine, my elbow against her sternum, blood washing over my wrist.

For a moment she held perfectly still, her eyes wide, then a scream issued from her lips that probably woke up old Bill across the street, and alerted every cop in the neighborhood, not that I gave a tinker's dam.

I let go of her and she stumbled away, blood erupting as if growing from the pale blue of her dress, visible beneath her open wool coat.

She found the door and staggered outside; I stayed with her to see that she did not remove the knife; she fell on her side and stained the snow, twitching. I stood there staring at her body, and I might be there still if I hadn't suddenly seen figures racing from across the street, and a few in the yard inside the fence. Some of them were holding pistols, and there were one or two rifles or shotguns.

I don't like shotguns.

Spotlights blasted their way to me as I stood by the door, and to Kellem, stretched out on the melting snow and mud of the lawn.

I slammed the door and shot the bolt, where I stood for just a moment, then I heard, distorted by distance, wood, and some sort of amplifier, *"You in there. This is the police. The house is surrounded. Come out slowly with your hands empty."*

Crap.

I yelled back. "The first cop through this door gets his head blown off," then I tried not to laugh. *You'll never take me alive, coppers.* Just call me Jimmy Cagney.

Jim said, "Why did you say that?"

"They think I'm armed and dangerous," I said. "Let them assume I have a gun."

"Why?"

"So they'll keep their distance while I figure out what to do."

I remembered then that I did, in fact, have a gun. Where was it? In the attic, next to the signboard with the red "R" on it. I could use the sign, too.

They called a few more ultimatums at me, but I was no longer listening. I turned to Susan, and yes, she was still breathing, and she was looking at me. Blood flowed from a wound in her throat, as if it had been ripped open by some sort of claw. Her left arm lay across her body at an unusual angle, and there seemed to be something wrong with the left side of her face. As I watched, she held out her right hand.

I took it, kissed her palm, and saw that she was dying. I think she knew it, too. She tried to speak, failed. I said, "It's all right, my love; I won't let them win. We will laugh at them all."

She tried to say something else, but didn't manage. She was going fast. I knew what I was going to have to do, and there was no point in waiting. I kissed her forehead, then her lips, then her eyes; and then I held her close and did what was necessary.

As I laid her down on the floor, Jim was standing there. "What now?" he said.

"Now? I don't know."

"You'd better get out of here," he said. "The police—"

"If they find Susan, they'll have her embalmed."

"So? Oh. I understand. Do you think she'd want—"
He broke off, seeing my face, then he looked away.

I studied her still form. "I do not want her to die,"
I said.

"What will you do?"

"Hide her, the same place I've been hiding."

"If they search—"

"Why should they? They don't know she's here."

"But they know you're in here."

"I won't be," I said.

"You're leaving?"

"Yes."

He nodded. "It might work," he said slowly. "You'll
have to let them see you leave."

"I know."

"You should hurry. The sun—"

"I know."

He frowned. "What bothers me," he said, "is that,
if they haven't caught you, if they know you're at large,
they're likely to search the house anyway."

"I know," I said. "I have a plan."

"What—?"

"Just let me think, all right?"

I dashed up to the attic and found the sign with the
"R," and the pistol. I set the sign in front of the one
nonboarded-up window. That, I hoped, would discour-
age tear gas; tear gas would annoy me.

The loudspeaker was still going outside, and it still
is, as I put these words on paper. They want me to
surrender. It is annoying, but that is all.

I took Susan to the vault, and laid her down com-
fortably, to rest until the time comes for her to rise. A
day, two days, a week, a month; it doesn't matter. They
won't find her, because they won't search, because there
will be nothing to search for—nothing they know about,
at any rate.

It has taken me longer to set this all down on paper than most of it took to happen; it is late now, and I am beginning to feel tired. As I look back on these words, it appears that I wrote this in one continuous stream; actually I have gotten up several times and walked around. The last time was when Jim came in. He said, "What are you going to do, Jack?"

I said, "Insure Susan's safety."

"How?"

I shrugged and went downstairs to look at Susan again. I cleaned up the wound in her throat; she looks pale and very beautiful. While I was down there I found my good coat; there is no longer any reason not to wear it, so I can go back to looking like my old natty self.

I can sense the false dawn in the east. The police are, no doubt, waiting for sunrise before they come in after me. I will save them the trouble.

No doubt the "Tac Group" is waiting for me, maybe expecting me to charge out at them, gun blazing. Who am I to disappoint them? They'll probably perform an autopsy. I wish I could stick around to find out what that will reveal. I wonder how they'll explain it, or if they'll bother trying. I wonder if they will even care.

I will leave this pile of papers, and my pendant, next to Susan, where she lies, even now, awaiting her birth into a new life.

I will step out into the dawn, and let them do as they will. I can think of nothing more to say, and I am feeling too weary to type in any case. The sun has risen. I feel the breeze through the boarded-up window; it is warm and fine, and I think there are no more clouds. Spring has come at last.

EPILOGUE

mor·al *adj.* 1. Of or concerned with the judgment of the goodness or badness of human action and character: pertaining to the discernment of good and evil . . . *n.* 1. The lesson or principle contained in or taught by a fable, story, or event. 2. A concisely expressed precept or general truth; maxim.

AMERICAN HERITAGE DICTIONARY

ttttttttttttttttttttttt
hghghghghghghghghghghghg
asdfghjkl

I am not used to manual typewriters. If typing becomes a chore, I shall simply stop. In fact, I don't know why I am doing it at all, except, now that I think of it, perhaps as a tribute to dear Jonathan. He must have spent hours up here, judging by the size of the stack of paper he left me. Perhaps I ought to read it.

It is odd that I don't miss him more than I do. I remember how he made me feel, but it seems so far away. Everything seems so far away. I remember how frightened I was while he held me, and I remember thinking that something must be wrong because there was no pain.

There is no pain now, but nothing is wrong.

Nothing is wrong at all.

I asked Jim what it all meant, but he wouldn't or

couldn't tell me. Jim is a dear man. I'd love to embrace him, but there is nothing to embrace. Perhaps I shall go out and enjoy the spring evening, and see if perhaps I can find someone I *can* embrace. Let me go back and underline that word. There. How splendid. There is something wonderfully engaging about letting one's thoughts flow out onto the page. I used to keep a diary. I wonder why I stopped.

It seems strange that I do not feel that I will miss anyone, or, for that matter, any thing. Anything? Any thing. What a pesky language. I should learn a few others, just for contrast.

I retain fond memories of Mother, and of Dad, and my brother, and Rick and Jenny, and a few others, but the notion that I'll not see them again doesn't bother me; and there is nothing that I own that is worth a thought. Isn't that odd? After all the hours I spent picking out— ah, but there's an idea. I shall sneak back into the house, and write a note saying that I am going on a long vacation, and I'll give all of my prints to Gillian, who was complaining about how bare her room was, now that she's taken down those hideous things she called paintings. I'll bet she'd like my prints. And I can ask her to send my records to Rick, and the rest they can give away as far as I'm concerned.

Jim says I should leave this town, at least for a while, because it could be a problem if I were to meet someone I know. I suppose Jim is right; he seems like a very wise man. I wish there were someone who could go with me, but maybe it is better this way. I've been alone before.

Where shall I go? There is a whole world, and all the time in it. I am tired of the Midwest. Perhaps I shall go to London. Or San Francisco. I've always wanted to see San Francisco.

But there is so much that I don't know how to do. I know that I must bring my resting place with me, but how to arrange for it? Maybe by train? It might be that, if I read through those papers of Jonathan's, I'll learn something useful. If not, it will be pleasant to hear his voice again; I still have that stack of poetry he gave me. And a piece of petrified wood. At least I think I do. Where did I put those things?

My fingers are getting tired from striking these keys, so I believe I shall stop now.